Paperboy

Paperboy

Vince Vawter

Text copyright © 2013 by Vince Vawter
Jacket art copyright © 2013 by Chris Sheban

Visit us on the Web! randomhouse.com/kids

Educators and librarians, for a variety of teaching tools,
visit us at RHTeachersLibrarians.com

Library of Congress Cataloging-in-Publication Data
Vawter, Vince.
Paperboy / Vince Vawter.—1st ed.
p.   cm.
Summary: When an eleven-year-old boy takes over a friend's newspaper route in July 1959, in Memphis, his debilitating stutter makes for a memorable month.
ISBN 978-0-385-74244-3 (hc)—ISBN 978-0-307-97505-8 (ebook)—
ISBN 978-0-375-99058-8 (glb)
[1. Stuttering—Fiction.   2. Newspaper carriers—Fiction.   3. Interpersonal relations—Fiction.   4. Self-esteem—Fiction.   5. Race relations—Fiction.
6. Family life—Tennessee—Fiction.   7. Memphis (Tenn.)—History—20th century—Fiction.]   I. Title.
PZ7.V4734Pap 2013
[Fic]—dc23   2012030546

The text of this book is set in 12-point Goudy.

Book design by Kenny Holcomb

Printed in the United States of America

10 9 8 7 6 5 4 3 2 1

First Edition

To the memory of my father,
Vilas V. Vawter Jr.

Paperboy

Chapter One

I'm typing about the stabbing for a good reason. I can't talk.

Without stuttering.

Plus I promised Mam I would never tell what happened to my yellow-handle knife. Mam might say that typing is cheating but I need to see the words on paper to make sure everything happened the way my brain remembers it. I trust words on paper a lot more than words in the air.

The funny way I talk is not so much like fat pigs in cartoons as I just get stuck on a sound and try to push the word out. Sometimes it comes out after a little pushing but other times I turn red in the face and lose my breath and get dizzy circles going around in my head. There's not much I can do about it except think of another word or keep on pushing.

The lady my parents hired to show me how to talk is teaching me to use a trick she calls Gentle Air which means letting out a little of my breath before getting stuck on a word. So when I feel like I'm going to have trouble saying a word I try to sneak up on it by making a hissing noise.

S-S-S-S.

When you're eleven years old it's better to be called a snake than a retard.

Some days if I've gotten stuck on a bunch of words at school I'll come home and put a piece of notebook paper in the typewriter that someone from my father's office brought to our house a long time ago and forgot to take back. The same one I'm typing these words on now. I peck out the words that gave me the most trouble for the day. My hands know where the letters are and I don't have to think up different tricks to help me push out a word.

I like the sound the typewriter key makes when it smacks the black ribbon because it's always the same. I never know what kinds of sounds are going to come out of my mouth. If anything happens to come out at all.

Just so you know. I hate commas. I leave them out of my typing any time I think I can get away with it. My composition teacher said a comma meant it was time for a pause. I pause all the time when I'm trying to talk whether I want to or not. Humongous pauses. I would rather type a gazillion *ands* than one little comma.

I type so much in my room that the white letters are wearing off the typewriter keys. But the key with the comma on it looks brand-new and it can stay that way if you ask me.

Mam came to Memphis from Mississippi when I was five to live with us and help take care of me and one thing's for sure. I wouldn't have made it this far without her.

Mam's real name is Miss Nellie Avent. My mother told me to call her Miss Nellie but that didn't work for me because of the *N* sound coming after the *M* sound. Mam was as close as I could come to saying her name and she allowed as how that suited her fine.

She said that we made a good pair because she couldn't write very well and I had the best handwriting she had ever seen for a little man. That's what she called me from the first day that she came to live with us. Little Man.

Mam is my best friend in all the world except when it comes to playing ball and then Rat takes over. His real name is Art.

He had it written in easy-to-read letters on his catcher's mitt on the first day of third grade but I had to nickname him Rat because the A sound wasn't going to come out of my mouth that day without giving me a bunch of trouble. He allowed as how Rat was okay with him and that made me like him from the start. He didn't even look like a rat but he understood quicker than most kids that Rat was the best I could do on his name because of the easy *R* sound. Mam calls him Mr. Rat which always cracks me up.

My stuttering probably makes me the best nicknamer in Memphis.

One of my hard baseball throws busted Rat in the mouth on the last day of sixth grade. That's the reason I told him I would handle his paper route for July so he could visit his grandparents on their farm outside Memphis. I didn't much want to take on the route but I thought I owed it to Rat for busting his lip. Rat says I show off too much with my hard throws and I guess he's right and I needed to pay for it.

The paper route was where I met all the new people in my life and where all the bad stuff happened. And some good stuff too. At least I think it was good. I'm still trying to figure all of it out and I'm hoping that putting the words on paper will help.

I knew I would like the throwing part of the paper route because throwing is what I do best. Baseballs. Rocks. Dirt clods. Newspapers. Anything.

But it was no big secret that the thing worrying me the most was collecting the money for the newspapers each week on Friday night.

The idea of going up to a house and ringing a doorbell was swelling my insides. The reason I hate talking to people who don't know me is because when they first see me I look like every other kid. Two eyes. Two arms. Two legs. Crew-cut hair. Nothing special. But when I open my mouth I turn into something else. Most people don't take the time to try to understand what's wrong with me and probably just figure I'm not right in the head. They try to get rid of me as fast as possible.

The best thing I could do when my insides got nervous was talk to Mam who lives over the garage in back of our house.

From our kitchen I saw that her light was still on. I knew she was probably reading her Bible except she really didn't read it as much as just look at it. She had taught me to say the twenty-third psalm with her and she would move her finger along the sentences but it never came out exactly even with the words we were saying.

I climbed the steps and knocked my special knock on her door. The one that sounds like Shave and a Haircut Two Bits.
    What you want, Little Man?
    s-s-s-s-Need to s-s-s-s-talk.
    We'll talk a spell but then you have to get back on to the house for bed.

Mam knew that collecting for the paper route was a heavy weight pushing down on me but she also knew that I liked to beat around the bush before talking about something important.
    s-s-s-s-Do you ever have a s-s-s-s-feeling that something bad is s-s-s-s-going to happen?

5

Some, Little Man. Where I growed up in Coldwater we had an old man who made a livin' out of telling the future.

s-s-s-s-Tell s-s-s-s-bout him.

This old man with a curly white beard told the future by pitching animal bones and then paying mind to how they landed. Folks said it was blasphemy to heed that beardy old man but he never told me wrong.

What s-s-s-s-did he s-s-s-s-tell?

He told me my elder brother was going to come to harm. That summer my brother John drowned in Coldwater Creek with not a teacup of water in it.

How s-s-s-s-did he s-s-s-s-drown?

Nobody knows. The doctor said they was more water in that sweet boy's lungs than in that ditch.

I finally got around to telling Mam that I thought I would like the throwing part of Rat's newspaper route but the collecting part on Friday nights was messing me up on my insides.

I'll go collectin' with you.

s-s-s-s-Need to s-s-s-s-do it on s-s-s-s-my own.

You be growing up, Little Man. I's proud of you.

Mam said she had to do a little more cleanup in the kitchen and that she would go back to the house with me. I knew the only reason she said that was because she wanted to make sure I didn't get too down in the dumps.

My father's Buick was coming up the drive as we went in the kitchen door. Mam waited for him and held open the door when she saw he was getting his big briefcases out of the backseat.

What you think about Little Man's paper route, Mr. V.?

My father looked at me and smiled.

I'm sure he'll throw those newspapers as well as he throws a baseball.

I had told my father earlier that I thought I might take on the route and he said it was good that I was going to help out a friend.

Mam and I went up the back stairs and down the hall past my mother who was putting white stuff on her face and things in her hair like she always did at night at the dresser in her bedroom.

Good night, sweetie.

I started to say good night back but I got stuck on the hard G and I knew if I ever got the G out the N would also give me trouble. So I just kept on walking down the hall to my room with my breath stuck in me and not feeling like fooling with a bunch of s-s-s-s tricks seeing as how it was at the end of the day and I was tired.

Mam put my dirty clothes and towels down the laundry chute when I had finished in the bathroom and then came to my room. She patted my foot when I got in bed and turned out the light on her way out.

Mam had stopped giving me goodnight kisses on the top of my head a long time ago without me asking. You never had to tell Mam what you were thinking like you did with regular grown-ups. She always knew on her own.

Chapter Two

On the first Monday of the route the regular carriers started getting to the newspaper drop a little before three o'clock.

I already had the two *Press-Scimitar* canvas bags hanging on a wooden fence in the alley like Rat had showed me.

Most of the carriers were about my age but a few grown-ups had routes which kept the kids from horsing around too much. I knew some of the guys from school but most were from parts of town I didn't know.

An older boy in cutoff jeans and a black T-shirt spread out his bags on the fence next to me.

Where's Art?

s-s-s-s-Gone . . . for s-s-s-s-July.

He looked at me funny. I was saying in my head that Rat was taking off the month of July so he could spend it on his granddaddy's farm. That's what I was thinking but I had to choose words that felt like they had some kind of a chance of coming out of my mouth. I always picked my way around words and sounds in sentences like I walked around broken bottles and dog turds in alleys.

Where's he gone to?

Saying *grandparents'* wasn't going to work. I could feel the G sound balling up in my throat when I just thought about saying the word.

Farm.

The word came out of my mouth without much of a pause or a hiss because I could slip up on the F sound if I went at it just right.

What farm?

Just then the white *Press-Scimitar* truck rolled into the alley and the back door opened. I moved to the truck to get the first bundles so I wouldn't have to keep talking to the kid.

With all my bundles in one spot I pulled out my yellow-handle knife to try to cut the heavy cords around the papers. The knife had a long single blade that was so dull I could close it on my finger and it wouldn't cut me. I had been meaning to have it sharpened because I didn't want to spend extra time sawing through the bundle cords and I didn't want anything slowing me down. Soon I had all my papers folded extra tight.

I had gone with Rat so many times that I was sure I knew all the houses but just to be safe I had his route book in the back pocket of my shorts.

In the part of Memphis where I live all the street names are sunk in the concrete on every corner in nice blue tile. I know all the streets but I like to read the name in my head each time I come to one. Vinton. Harbert. Carr. Melrose. Goodbar. Peabody.

The streets are like friends that I don't have to talk to.

The teacher my parents hired to help me talk had given me some drills to work on during summer recess. She explained that I had extra trouble with words that started with a B sound or a P sound because those words meant I had to put my lips together and let the air build up a little inside my mouth.

She said the problem was that my lips tightened like a clenched fist and the air couldn't get through. The more I tried to say words that started with B and P the tighter my lips would close up on me.

My plan for practicing the drills was to try to say a hard word just before I threw a paper on a porch. It was a kind of a game choosing the words and then hearing them come out of my mouth as I chunked a *Press-Scimitar*.

I had picked out a good word to say at the next house on Harbert. The two-story was white brick with thick hedges growing up over the porch railing. I didn't want to take a chance on throwing the paper in the tall bushes so I walked up close to toss it underhanded and in a normal voice I said

Pitch.

A chain on a porch swing clanked and soon a lady in a green house-coat was standing at the top of the porch steps with one hand on her hip and looking straight at me. Her other hand held a glass with ice in it. She had long red hair that was piled up on her head every which way. Her legs were spread out wide on the porch like she was taking a lead off first base. The way she was standing didn't let the flaps of her housecoat cover her up like they should have been doing. She wasn't wearing shoes.

What did you call me, young man?

I felt like turning and running but my legs wouldn't move. Much less my mouth. The lady walked down the porch steps.

I heard you call me a bitch.

I stood in the yard shaking my head side to side.

Don't shake your head at me, young man, and tell me you didn't.

She moved toward me with the glass in her hand. She swirled the glass around and around which made the ice cubes clink. I had never seen her before even though she only lived a few streets over from me. I couldn't remember the customer's name from Rat's route book.

What's the matter with you? Can't you talk?

The red-haired lady stared and made sure that I knew she wasn't going away until I gave her an answer.

s-s-s-s-Just s-s-s-s-p

I had made a mistake to try to say *practicing*. A bad *P* word for me. I started over.

s-s-s-s-Just s-s-s-s-rehearsing saying s-s-s-s-words.

My answer was so soft I wasn't sure she heard me.

What? Rehearsing? Calling me a bitch?

My head kept shaking from side to side like one of those brown toy dogs in the back windows of cars.

s-s-s-s-Not what s-s-s-s-I said ma'am. Sorry.

She moved back from me one step and almost lost her balance. Her housecoat flopped open again.

Where's my regular paperboy?

s-s-s-s-Rat's on the s-s-s-s-farm.

I heard the words come out of my mouth but they sounded like I had just told the red-haired lady that somewhere in the world there were a bunch of rats running around on somebody's farm. Even when I managed to say words halfway decent they didn't always have the meaning I intended.

Are you the boy who walks with his colored maid to the bus stop?

I nodded.

s-s-s-s-Just helping my s-s-s-s-friend with his s-s-s-s-route. s-s-s-s-Didn't say what you s-s-s-s-thought.

I should hope not.

The glass in her hand looked like it held only ice water at first but when she had moved closer I smelled the whiskey.

Now you listen to me.

She stepped toward me and raised her finger. I was hoping she wouldn't lose her balance again.

Don't throw the newspaper AT my house. Walk up and place the paper in front of the dwo-o—or like a gentleman.

Somehow she had managed to put a *W* in *door*.

I nodded extra hard. She studied me like she wanted me to say something else but I was clean out of words. I backed away from the house onto the sidewalk and kept going down Harbert.

My T-shirt was soaked with sweat and my khaki shorts looked like I had taken a bath in them. From then on I just walked up to the porches and tossed the papers underhanded. You can bet I didn't practice any more word drills.

By the time I had thrown my last newspaper for the day I had come up with a good plan. I ran all the way home and up the back stairs to my room. I put a clean sheet of notebook paper in the typewriter.

The big attic fan was roaring and a good breeze was blowing through my window. I checked the name on Harbert in Rat's route book. I typed slow and careful so I didn't have to go back and rub out any letters.

Dear Mrs. Worthington,

This is a note from your substitute paperboy that you talked to in your yard today. I am very sorry that I caused you alarm. I was practicing my speech drills while I was throwing your paper. It might have sounded like I said a bad word. But I didn't. I am very sorry and I promise to put your paper exactly where you want it for the rest of July. I will also tell your real paperboy where to put it. Please let me know if I can do anything else for you for the next month. Thank you very much.

Your Substitute Paperboy

Inside my head I said each word over and over. I folded the piece of paper in half and then in half again. On the outside I printed Mrs. Worthington's address with a sharp pencil.

1396 Harbert

I ran to the house on Harbert and checked to see that Mrs. Worthington wasn't still on the porch swing and then clothespinned the note to the black letterbox at the side of her front door.

The rest of the week stayed hot but by Thursday I had the route down to about two hours.

At 1396 Harbert I was just getting ready to lay the paper on the porch in the perfect spot when I saw Mrs. Worthington peeking out at me through the glass of her front door. She opened the door and walked out on the porch wearing a bright green dress with a big shiny black belt.

I didn't usually pay much attention to dresses that ladies wore but this one looked special the way the wide belt fastened tight around her middle like it was dividing her into two parts.

That first day Mrs. Worthington had looked about the same age as my mother but she looked younger this time. Almost as young as Rat's sister who was still in college.

Mrs. Worthington had on bright red lipstick that made her smile look bigger than it really was. She had figured out a way to make her eyelashes longer and she had a green color on her eyelids that came close to matching her dress. When she talked I watched her red lips move like it was the first time I had ever seen words come out of a person's mouth.

Young man, don't think me rude but you startled me when you came by earlier this week.

When she said the word *Startled* her voice went higher like she wanted me to pay extra attention to the word but I was already concentrating double hard on everything she said.

With a lot of Gentle Air coming out of my mouth in front of almost every word I told her that everything was my fault and she sure didn't owe me an apology. She said she liked the note I had written and that she thought her husband might know my father because they both worked downtown in the same building.

Doesn't your father fly his own airplane?

s-s-s-s-Yes ma'am. s-s-s-s-But only a s-s-s-s-little one.

Have you flown in it?

s-s-s-s-Some.

I thought about saying A Gazillion Times but I didn't want to try to make the G sound and saying *gazillion* to Mrs. Worthington didn't seem right anyway.

Would you care to join me for a lemonade?

s-s-s-s-Need to keep s-s-s-s-going.

Deep down I was feeling I wanted to stay and talk to her but my talking was working out good compared to my first day with Mrs. Worthington and I didn't want to take a chance on spoiling things.

Will you be coming by Friday evening?

I remembered from Rat's collection book that 1396 Harbert was scheduled to pay monthly. Stepping around hard words I tried to explain to Mrs. Worthington how collecting was supposed to work.

You s-s-s-s-pay by the s-s-s-s-month. s-s-s-s-Not each week.

She smiled and then did something that surprised me. She touched me on the nose with her pointing finger and kept it there and then she pushed on it like she was ringing a doorbell.

I think I'll start paying weekly. Easier for me to keep track of, sweetie.

s-s-s-s-Be happy to s-s-s-s-come by on s-s-s-s-Friday.

See you tomorrow then, sweetie.

I had gone from being yelled at to being called Sweetie all in the same week. The way she said Sweetie was nothing like how my mother said it. Mrs. Worthington seemed like a different lady the second time I saw her. A very pretty lady.

On the way home I started wishing that Mam's fortune-teller man from Coldwater was around to throw some bones and tell me what Mrs. Worthington was all about and why I wanted so much to see her again.

Chapter Three

My favorite place to read in the summer is outside on the covered brick patio in our backyard sitting on the Wicked Furniture.

Rat was at our house a couple of years ago when a truck delivered the new white furniture my parents had bought on a trip to New Orleans. My mother asked Rat if he liked our wicker furniture and Rat asked me later what made the furniture Wicked.

I spelled out for Rat the right way to say it but he said he liked Wicked better. I've called it Wicked ever since because it's easier for me to say it that way. I get upset when other people use the wrong words since it's so easy for most everybody to make any sound they want. I guess I should be mad at myself for substituting Wicked for Wicker but you can always count on me to take the easy way out when it comes to getting words out of my mouth.

I was trying to read a book about Babe Ruth that my father had brought me from his last trip out of town but I was having a hard time thinking about what was on the pages. The first night of collecting was only a few hours away. It was pushing down on me like a history test I hadn't studied enough for. I didn't know if I was going to have the guts to ring a doorbell and wait for somebody to come to the door and then make the hard *P* sound that started *paperboy*.

About that time a cart came jangling down the alley. It sounded like Ara T's cart with all the bits and pieces of metal clanking on it. Ara T was a junkman who pushed his cart up and down the alleys and did odd jobs for white people. Ara T could whet a knife or a pair of scissors razor-sharp.

Just about any doodad that Ara T could find on the street that had a shine to it or made a noise ended up nailed on his pushcart that was made from pieces of scrap wood and old bicycle wheels. I unlatched the fence gate and went into the alley even though Mam had told me that she didn't like me hanging around Ara T.

How do, Little Man?

Ara T probably had heard Mam call me that because he was all the time picking through cans behind our house. I pulled my knife from my front pocket and handed it to him.

s-s-s-s-Needs sharpening.

He took the knife and flicked open the blade and pushed up the sleeve of his old coat and dragged the knife across the curly hairs on his arm. Even in the middle of summer Ara T wore a heavy coat.

20

Mam always said she could smell Ara T coming before she heard him and if you couldn't smell him and his stinking coat you could smell the Bugler tobacco that he made into cigarettes by licking thin pieces of paper he kept in the top pocket of his coat. The cigarettes in his mouth always looked like they had been chewed on more than they had been smoked. He never bothered to take the cigarette out of his mouth like most grown-ups did so when he wanted to blow smoke he would just use the other side of his mouth and then keep puffing.

Sure do. This knife won't do for hot butter.

He made a big show out of feeling around in his coat pockets.

My whetstone's at my place but I can have your knife for you directly.

Ara T stood looking at me with my knife in his hand. He turned it over and over like he was studying both sides of the blade.

s-s-s-s-Don't need it till s-s-s-s-tomorrow.

We stood staring at each other. Ara T ran his thumb back and forth across the blade.

I's needin' me some oil to whet with. Advance me some coin for a smite of a can.

I always had a bunch of money in the desk drawer in my room. When my father came home from his trips he would wink and ask me if the bank was open and then empty all the coins from his pocket into the drawer. He also gave me paper dollars when I swept leaves off the patio or cleaned the mud off his hunting boots. Rat's father also paid me sometimes to untangle the rolls of chain and rope at his hardware store. He said I was the best he had ever seen at untangling things. I liked doing it. At least if I couldn't untangle my words I could get something else straightened out. I had never bothered counting the money but the drawer was getting heavy from all the coins in it.

I ran up to my room and got two quarters and came back out to the alley.

Little Man's gonna be rollin' in dough now with that paper route.

I smiled at him and nodded.

I wondered if Ara T had seen me throwing papers during the week. I didn't remember seeing him. I handed him the two quarters. He tipped his dirty hat and put the quarters along with my knife in the front pocket of his pants that looked at least two sizes too big for him and were held up by the same kind of brown cord that wrapped the newspaper bundles.

Have it for you directly, Little Man.

I knew I would get a sharp knife back. Ara T showed Rat and me in the alley one time how he could cut a tin can into a ribbon with a knife he had sharpened. That can looked like the peel of an apple after he got through with it.

I watched Ara T push his cart on down the alley. He looked to the left and right in case there was something that caught his eye. He took the lids off garbage cans and poked around and checked all the bottles to see if anything was left in them.

Mam had told me I shouldn't hang around Ara T because he sometimes got the fits but Rat and I had never seen him do anything but push his cart and pick up junk and do odd jobs. I liked all the colored junkmen who pushed their carts around our neighborhood because they minded their own business and just nodded at me when they passed and that meant I didn't have to go to the trouble of trying to figure out how to say something.

I had decided to wear long pants instead of my regular shorts for the first Friday night of collecting. If I started stuttering when people answered the doorbell at least I would look more grown-up doing it with my legs covered.

I had planned my collecting route to go up Vinton across Bellevue to the smaller houses and then come back down Harbert toward my house. Mrs. Worthington's house would be the last before I headed over to Rat's to turn in the money to his mother. I was saving the best for last. I had been thinking more about seeing Mrs. Worthington again.

The first five houses on my list had their envelopes stuck in the screen door or clipped on the letterbox just like everything was supposed to work. The sixth house at 1219 Vinton was my first doorbell.

I had never before in my life walked up on a front porch to call a stranger to their door.

I heard the bell through the screen door when I pushed the button. The sound made my insides jump. I never liked to hear the doorbell ring at my house because it meant I might have to talk to somebody besides Mam and Rat.

A kid a little younger than me was sitting in the living room in front of a TV set so close that he could touch it. The sound was off. He didn't move a muscle when the doorbell rang. A man in a tie and white shirt started toward the door with the newspaper in his hand and then stopped when he saw me.

I think it's the paperboy, hon. Where's his envelope?

A voice from the back of the house said she had forgotten how much it was and to ask me. The man walked to the screen door.

How much, son?

I knew exactly how much. Ninety-five cents. But the word *ninety* was just as tough for me to say as a *P* word because my tongue would hit the roof of my mouth and stick there without any sound coming out. I reached for Rat's collection book and pencil trying to look like I was checking on something. I was thinking about saying Sixty cents because of the easy *S* sound on both words but I would be losing money if I did that. I also thought about rounding it off by saying One dollar but people could accuse me of cheating them out of a nickel.

I finally came up with something that I didn't like to do much because people looked at me funny but sometimes the trick worked in school. I tossed my stubby pencil in the air with my right hand. The instant I flipped the pencil s-s-s-s-Ninety-five cents eased out of my

24

mouth. The only problem was that when I tossed something I usually got nervous and dropped whatever I was flipping. The pencil hit the concrete porch and the point broke.

The man opened the screen door.
Here's a buck for you.

Mam had reminded me to take some coins with me from my desk drawer to make change. I reached in my pocket for a nickel and offered it to him.
Keep it, son.

He turned away and I watched him walk back into the dark of the house with only the light of the TV showing.

My first doorbell of the night had gone better than I had expected. I had gotten my first tip and I was feeling a little better about the collecting. The biggest problem was that I had broken the point off my pencil and I didn't have my knife to sharpen it.

Walking the route in the afternoon and throwing the papers was nothing new to me but walking late in the day when the sun was going down was all different. The big trees blocked what little sun was left and the houses somehow seemed bigger. House lights were coming on everywhere and families were usually talking around the dinner table or watching TV. I eased up on each porch that was on my weekly collection list and hoped with all my heart that the owners had remembered to put their envelopes out.

I had reached the farthest point on the route. The next collection was at one of the small houses on Vance where the man with the funny name lived. Mr. Spiro.

Rat said Mr. Spiro was all the time stopping his paper for a month or two when he would go on trips. Rat also said that he was a nice enough old guy but that he used weird words when he talked. But he always had the exact change and most of the time was good for a small tip. Rat also said that Mr. Spiro would invite him to come in if the weather was cold or wet but Rat always told people it was against newspaper rules to go inside houses. I think that was just a polite way of saying no because Rat's parents had made him promise that he would never go into anybody's house on the route.

The front porch light was on even though it wasn't all-the-way dark yet. I rang the bell and waited. I was counting on Mr. Spiro to have his ninety-five cents ready so I wouldn't have to try to say those words again.

The wooden door with the small pane of glass at the top opened. Mr. Spiro wore glasses that dropped down on his nose and his head was bald except for a little gray hair around his ears that was cut short. He held two big books. One in each hand. His fingers were stuffed inside to mark his place.

Hello, Mr. Reliever. How are you this glorious summer eve?

s-s-s-s-Okay.

I think I have ninety-five percent of a US dollar right here for you. Just one moment.

Mr. Spiro used words in strange ways but it was easy enough to tell what he was talking about. He made what he said sound important like he was talking to a grown-up. I liked him double when I knew I wouldn't have to try to say Ninety-five cents again.

He put his books down on a table near the door and was careful to keep them open to where his fingers had been marking his place. He counted out the coins and dropped them into my hand.

I thought I was home free at this address but then he asked me the one question I dreaded most in all the world. The question that always locked my neck like when a bigger kid on the playground gets you in a headlock.

He asked me my name.

Young man, before we complete our transaction I need to be apprised of your name. Young Arthur forgot to relay that important bit of information to me last week.

What Mr. Spiro couldn't have known was that asking me to say my name out loud was like asking me to recite the Gettysburg Address. My history teacher had tried to make me do that but he finally let me write it out in longhand after it took me about half the class to get out Four Score and Seven Years Ago and with all the kids snickering at every word I tried to say.

For some reason saying my name was the hardest thing of all for me to do. It didn't start with a *B* or *P* but it was a sound that refused to budge inside me no matter how much Gentle Air I piled on it. And to make matters worse my first and last name started with the same sound. I hated trying to say my full name more than I hated anything in the world. Including commas.

I reached in my sweaty pocket for my pencil but most of the time a pencil toss didn't help when trying to get my mouth to make the sounds that started my name. My throat was already tightening up and air was getting hard to come by. I couldn't find the pencil anyway because my hands were shaking. My throat and my stomach knotted up tighter when I thought again about the sound. I put my top row of teeth to my bottom lip to try to push it out. Nothing. I pushed harder. Nothing. I jerked with my right hand to pretend I was tossing a pencil but by that time I was out of breath.

Mr. Spiro stood there waiting on me. Smiling and looking straight at me just like Mam always did.

The only thing to do was to make another run at the sound by taking another deep breath and starting over. The thought of another breath tightened me even more and so against all good reason and against my teacher's rules I held my breath and continued to try to push out the sound with all my might.

The last thing I remember was seeing a fly buzzing around Mr. Spiro's porch light. The light got brighter and brighter and the fly got bigger and bigger. As big as my father's airplane and buzzing just as loud. Then the porch light and all lights everywhere went out at the same time like when a big lightning storm hit our neighborhood.

When I came back to my senses I was sitting on Mr. Spiro's porch with my back against the wooden planks of his house and the coins he had dropped in my hand scattered everywhere.

Mr. Spiro held one wet rag on my head and dabbed at my lips with another one that was splattered with blood. He was squatting down beside me and he had this big smile on his face. He wasn't laughing but you would have thought he had just finished watching Sid Caesar on TV. I couldn't figure out what he could be smiling about.

Feeling a tad better?

I nodded.

I'm going inside to get additional wet rags. I want you to sit right here and think about how well you are going to pitch in your next game.

He got up from his catcher's squat easily. I couldn't tell how old Mr. Spiro was but he was in good shape. His forearms were almost as big as my thighs and I had pretty big thighs for a kid my age.

How did Mr. Spiro know I was a pitcher? The night couldn't get any more upside down. Mr. Spiro came back to the porch and handed me more wet rags.

Let me see if I can recount the recent events. You simply nod your head if I'm correct.

Mr. Spiro talked in a voice that let you know he was getting down to business. He folded his big arms across his chest. I watched him from the corner of my eyes and never saw him blink.

When I asked your name a moment ago your inability to produce that sound due to your speech impediment caused you to interrupt your normal breathing pattern.

He sounded official like he was calling a baseball game on the radio.

You held on too long trying to make the sound and while doing so you bit into your lower lip.

I dabbed my lip. The bleeding had almost stopped.

You then fainted from lack of oxygen and the sudden rigidity of your muscles. Do I have all that correct?

I nodded.

His big arms reached out and lifted me like I was a little kid.

Let's get off the porch floor and sit on the swing. However, we shan't swing.

I had never heard anyone say *Shan't* but I knew it was short for *Shall Not*. I loved contractions as much as I hated commas because when two words were rolled into one it meant there was one less word to stutter on.

The way Mr. Spiro talked to me was exactly the way Mam talked even though the words they used were different. They both looked straight at me and made me feel like I belonged right where I was.

30

My head had cleared and the flies buzzing around the light fixture on the porch were back to regular fly size.

s-s-s-s-Need to s-s-s-s-go.

I pushed out the Gentle Air and the three words in such a whisper that I wasn't sure Mr. Spiro heard me.

Yes. I'm sure you do. But I'm going to suggest we sit on this swing a while longer to make certain you have your feet properly under you.

Not only did I like how he used words but I also liked how deep his voice was and how he made his words come out so even.

You don't have to talk while we rest here. In fact you probably won't be able to get a word in because I can easily hold forth for the two of us.

Mr. Spiro made a little laughing sound under his breath.

I'm an old man with too much time on his hands and not many people to have dialogue with. You don't need to worry about your lip there but your ears may drop off from being bombarded with my words.

Smiling was the last thing I felt like doing after almost biting through my lip but I couldn't help myself with Mr. Spiro talking in his radio voice.

Firstly, let me guess that you are probably a little embarrassed by what just occurred. No need, Young Traveler. We all have our deficits but no ledger will be tallied here.

I didn't understand the words exactly but I knew what he meant. I nodded.

Secondly, you also are concerned that I may think less of you because you cannot readily enunciate your name.

Mr. Spiro was looking straight at me and the way he was talking made me want to look straight into his eyes even though my speech teacher said I had the bad habit of not looking at people when they talked.

Let me share with you, my Young Messenger of the News, exactly how I judge thee.

He sounded like he was reading from Mam's Bible.

I know you to be a good friend of Young Arthur's. By the by, Young Arthur says you have more velocity on your fastball than anyone in the sixth grade.

Mr. Spiro made like he was holding a baseball in a two-fingered grip.

And while Young Arthur is proud to be called your catcher, methinks he is more proud to call you his friend. Thus, all that is vital to know is that you have won and continue to earn the friendship and respect of a fellow traveler. That constitutes the tote and sum in my book.

Like I told you. I understood what Mr. Spiro was saying even though I had never heard anyone talk like that. His words felt extra important by the way he said them. And he didn't call Rat a Hind Catcher. Rat always hated that.

We sat on the swing without talking for a while longer and then Mr. Spiro got to his feet.

Alas. You seem to be recovering at good speed. I'm sure you need to be on your way but permit me to step inside my berth for a moment.

I didn't know what time it was but I knew I was going to have a tough time beating it home by seven o'clock. It wasn't pitch-dark yet but more flies were swarming around the porch light and a few lightning bugs were warming up out in the yard for a big Friday night in Memphis.

Mr. Spiro returned with what looked like a corner of a dollar bill and sat down again beside me on the swing. On the George Washington side of the piece of the bill was a word hand-lettered in black ink.

Student

Mr. Spiro put the piece of the dollar bill in my hand along with the ninety-five cents he had scraped up from the porch floor.

Consider this slip of paper your extra compensation for this week. You have three more weeks to claim your golden fleece in its entirety.

I stood to go and thought I should say something or even shake Mr. Spiro's hand.

Now, Young Traveler, be off with the wind.

The way Mr. Spiro talked made me think I was part of a ceremony.

s-s-s-s-Thanks.

You are more than welcome.

I walked out of Mr. Spiro's yard and once I was out of his sight I started running down Vance and then turned onto Harbert. When I was nervous after I did some bad talking the best thing for me to do was run until there was no more breath in me.

I came to 1396 Harbert hoping there might be an envelope clothes-pinned on the door or the letterbox. There was no porch light on. I walked up the steps and rang the bell not knowing if I could get Paperboy out of my mouth if Mrs. Worthington came to the door. I wanted to see her in her green dress even if I couldn't say anything. I rang the bell again. No answer.

I started for Rat's house feeling like I do whenever an umpire calls off our ball game because the field is too wet.

Rat's mother saw that my lip was swollen but she didn't ask what had happened when I handed her the night's collection. Rat's mother was nice but I could tell that she was one of those grown-ups who always was uncomfortable talking to me.

When I got home I could see Mam in the kitchen. I didn't want Mam or my parents to see my busted lip so instead of going in the kitchen door I went in the outside back door that led to the back stairs.

In my room I looked harder at the corner of the dollar bill. I saw that the word *student* was printed in a careful hand. I guessed that Mr. Spiro had written the word. I wondered if he kept parts of dollar bills lying around his house with words hand-lettered on them. I decided to put the piece of a dollar in my leather billfold that my father had brought me from one of his trips. I kept it in my desk drawer along with my wristwatch that I had stopped wearing after a friend of my mother's asked me what time it was and I couldn't say it and the man thought I was an ignoramus who couldn't tell time. I liked the watch because it had the kind of metal band that slipped over my hand but all it was good for was to put around my billfold.

While I was at my desk my mother called from the hall that she and my father were going out to eat with friends and that Mam was cooking fried chicken for me.

I changed shirts and went down to the kitchen. Mam was putting a big plate of chicken on the table.

Law me, Little Man. How'd you bust that lip?

I told Mam I tripped over a curb trying to get home before dark. I didn't lie to Mam very often because I knew she would catch me quicker than most grown-ups.

Wants me to cut some chicken off the bone for you?

s-s-s-s-Takes more than s-s-s-s-bus . . . more than a s-s-s-s-fat lip to s-s-s-s-keep me away from your s-s-s-s-chicken.

Mam smiled because she knew I used up a lot of words to try to pay her a compliment. I ate three pieces.

Mam was working in the kitchen when my parents got back home from eating out. I went to the top of the stairs to try to hear what they were talking about. My mother started telling Mam what to order from the grocery and what to cook for the week. Mam never wrote anything down but she could remember every little thing my mother told her.

I heard Mam open the pantry door to put away her apron and then my father came into the kitchen.

Good night, Nellie.

Mr. V., if you see that junkman Ara T hanging 'round here be sure and lets me know.

Sure, Nellie. Which one is he?

He be the tall one always in a coat and hat and has the most junk fixed to his cart.

What's the problem?

I knows him a little and I just don't trust that man to leave stuff alone.

I think I know the one you're talking about. I'll keep an eye out. By the way, Nellie, how do you think our boy did on his first night of collecting?

I reckon all right, Mr. V. He ate him a big supper.

Sleep was a hard time coming after what had happened on Mr. Spiro's porch and I couldn't figure out why Mam was so down on Ara T.

I watched the shadows on the ceiling that cars made with their headlights when they came down the street. I didn't much like talking to strangers but I wanted to talk to Mr. Spiro again and to Mrs. Worthington. I thought about the first time I had seen her in her green housecoat with the flaps that she couldn't keep closed. But the thing that kept me awake the most that night was that I wouldn't have any way to cut the cords off my bundles on Saturday if Ara T didn't have my knife ready.

That meant I would have to ask another carrier to borrow his. And that meant saying Knife.

Chapter Four

A rainy Saturday morning in the summer was usually a good time to stay in bed and think about playing baseball but I was up and dressed early just like it was a school day.

Even though there was a light rain coming down I could hear a gasoline lawn mower in the front yard. A man always came on Saturday in the summer to cut our grass and trim our bushes. But not just any man.

Big Sack was the tallest and widest human being in Memphis. He would pull up to the curb in front of our house in his old truck and lift the mower out of the back like it was a feather. After he finished mowing he would come to the front door and ring the bell. Mam would give him his pay and he would be on his way without saying much.

I had asked Mam why he was called Big Sack.

His family name be Thomas but I don't rightly know his given name. The story always be told that when he came out of his mammy somebody yelled to get a clean flour sack from the kitchen and to make it a Big Sack.

Mam was sweeping the kitchen floor when I came downstairs. My father always played golf early on Saturday mornings with his business friends and I didn't know where my mother was but I could see her car was gone.

Can you eat flapjacks with your lip?

You s-s-s-s-bet I s-s-s-s-can.

Mam put down the broom and started getting the makings out of the pantry. About that time the front doorbell rang. She reached into her apron.

Go give Big Sack his three dollars.

When I went in the entrance hall Big Sack was standing at the front door that was mostly glass. His body blocked out the light coming in. I opened the door and handed him the three dollars. I was about to close the door when he took his hat off.

Reckon I could speak to Miss Nellie?

Sure. I'll s-s-s-s-get her.

Mam was finishing up the pancakes in the kitchen.

s-s-s-s-Big Sack s-s-s-s-needs you.

Start buttering your cakes. I be right back.

I was pouring syrup on my pancakes when Mam came into the kitchen. She sat down at the table across from me and gave me one of her straight looks that meant she had some business with me.

You been talkin' to Ara T?

I s-s-s-s-loaned him some s-s-s-s-quarters to s-s-s-s-buy—

Mam usually let me finish my sentences no matter how long it took me but she was ready to get on to me but good.

You know you're not supposed to be hanging 'round that man.

s-s-s-s-I ran in-s-s-s-s-to him in s-s-s-s-alley and—

Don't you be running into him. You hear me? You best be running the other way.

s-s-s-s-What's so s-s-s-s-bad about Ara T?

We're not talking 'bout that man no more. You stay away from him. Far away.

Mam hardly ever talked down about anyone but she never had anything good to say about Ara T. I asked her once if she had known him before she came to Memphis and all she said was As Little As I Could.

The first thing Mam would do if anything went missing in the neighborhood was to say she was going to check out Ara T and his junk cart. The reason I have my new Schwinn Black Phantom is because my old one with the big shiny headlight on the handlebars was stolen one night when I forgot to roll it in the garage. A while later Ara T showed up with a pushcart with new wheels on it. Mam said she checked the cart out but the wheels and tires didn't look like the ones from my stolen bike. Mam said that didn't mean Ara T couldn't have swapped wheels with another junkman from another part of town. Mam said she trusted Ara T about as far as she could heave him.

I pitched two innings that morning until the umpire called off the game because of the wet field. No one had gotten a hit off me yet so stopping the game usually would have bothered me but I had the paper route on my mind.

The newspaper truck came at one o'clock on Saturdays. Two hours earlier than the other days. The rain had slacked off to a drizzle.

While I was waiting on my bundles I saw Ara T a few houses down in the alley where he was checking garbage cans. There was no mistaking Ara T's cart with everything from broken toy guns to old car mirrors fastened to it. An old doll's head was tacked to the front. The handles of the cart were wrapped with different kinds of wire and cord.

I walked up to Ara T and stood by the metal garbage cans he was picking his way through. I was going to get my knife back and then I was going to mind Mam and stay away from him.

s-s-s-s-Got my s-s-s-s-k . . . ? My . . . s-s-s-s-k . . . ? s-s-s-s-Got my s-s-s-s-yellow handle?

He didn't turn around even though I was sure he had heard me. I stepped closer and changed to a louder voice.

s-s-s-s-You s-s-s-s-got it?

Still not paying any attention to me he rooted around in one of the cans he had already gone through. Then he swung around and gave me a mean stare like a teacher did when somebody was acting up in class.

Can't have it, boy, till you calls it what it is.

I smiled at first because I thought he may have been just kidding with me but any time Ara T came close to smiling you could see his gold tooth. I didn't see any gold. He was puffing on his crooked cigarette and trying to make like I wasn't there.

s-s-s-s-Do you s-s-s-s-have it?

Told you, boy. Can't have it till you call its name proper.

Ara T moved on to another bunch of cans behind the next house. Still not looking my way. I stood in the middle of the alley with my newspaper bags in my hand. Ara T wanted me to say Knife. I didn't know what game Ara T was playing but I didn't like it. I thought about yelling KNIFE at the top of my lungs because I never stuttered when I said words in a yell.

But Ara T moved on down the alley.

The carriers had started leaving on their routes. I waited until everyone was gone and then took my bundles over to my bags hanging on the fence. Picking my way along the alley I found an old tin can with a jagged top that wasn't rusted too bad. I twisted on the top until it came off and then took it to my bundles to start sawing on the heavy bundle cords as best I could. I decided I should have just kept my knife because even a dull knife that wouldn't cut butter was better than using the top of a tin can.

I knew if I told Mam that Ara T had my knife and wouldn't give it back that she would search him out and get my knife back in nothing flat. But I couldn't tell Mam I had talked to Ara T again. Anyway. If I was going to be collecting and handling the route on my own then I needed to start figuring how to solve my own problems.

Throwing papers wasn't any fun in the yellow raincoat Mam made me wear but I wasn't in so much of a hurry because it was Saturday.

More people were out on their porches on weekend afternoons and they gave me some big waves when I threw their papers that slid right up to their doors. I figured the route would take me to only a little after three o'clock.

On Vinton I walked up to the house where I had made my first collection the night before. The father and mother and a little girl were sitting in chairs out on the porch. Instead of making a throw I skipped up the steps to hand the paper to the father who had tipped me a nickel. As I passed the screen door I took a quick peek inside and there was TV Boy with his face stuck in front of the screen with the sound turned off just like the night before. How could TV Boy be so interested in something that took him away from the world like that? I could sit in front of my window sometimes and get lost staring out into space but the tiniest noise would usually bring me back to earth.

The times I sat down and watched television I found myself thinking about everything except what was happening on the screen.

Like on *The Howdy Doody Show*. When Howdy Doody was talking to Buffalo Bob I would forget what they were saying and start pretending that I was a puppet and wishing that somebody would pull the strings to make my mouth move so I didn't stutter. One time I didn't hear my mother when she came into the room and I was moving my mouth up and down like Howdy Doody with my hands over my head like I was pulling the strings. It must have scared her because she grabbed me by the shoulders and shook me and told me never to do that again.

My favorite person on the show was Clarabell the Clown. He couldn't talk but all he had to do to answer a question was honk the horn on a box he wore on the front of his clown suit. Buffalo Bob always knew exactly what Clarabell was saying with his horn. I could usually tell myself by the way he honked. I could tell if it was a quick happy honk or a long sad honk. Sometimes if I've had a bad stuttering day I'll start thinking how good it would be if I just had a horn to honk. Me honking the horn all the time would look stupid but not as stupid as some of the things I did when I tried to say words.

I stopped watching *The Howdy Doody Show* when I started playing baseball. It was better for me to spend time practicing my pitching instead of figuring out how to honk like a clown.

The drizzle had almost stopped when I got to Mr. Spiro's house on Vance. I couldn't tell if he was home because there was never a car in the driveway and he usually kept his front door closed even in the summer. I wanted to thank him for taking care of me after I bit into my lip trying to say my name but I really didn't feel like standing in that same spot again on the porch. Whenever I stuttered a lot in a certain spot I tried never to stand there again.

A good idea came to me. I would write him a short note and stick it inside his Saturday newspaper.

The only piece of paper to write on was a blank page from Rat's collection book. I sat down on a stoop across the street and sharpened the point of my pencil by rubbing it back and forth across the concrete. The page was small so I wrote in my smallest hand.

Dear Mr. Spiro,

Thank you for helping me when I did that dumb thing last night. I like the way you talk to me. Thank you for the piece of that dollar bill you gave me.

Your Substitute Paperboy

I put the page from the collection book into the fold of Mr. Spiro's newspaper and laid the newspaper on the porch in front of his door.

Mrs. Worthington's house was going to be the last house on my route for the day. Just the way I had planned.

A blue Ford I had never seen was in her driveway but it was worth taking a chance on ringing the bell. If she came to the door I had figured out a way to say that I was collecting for the night before when she wasn't at home. My pencil was in my hand in case I needed to make another emergency pencil toss to start a word.

I rang the doorbell and waited and was almost ready to leave a newspaper and walk on home when I saw somebody through the thin curtain over the glass door. He looked at me for a bit from back in the house and then walked to the door and opened it.

Help ya?

The man had a cigarette hanging from his lips and was in his stocking feet. I had only seen Mr. Worthington once or twice and he had always been in a suit and tie but this guy didn't look like Mr. Worthington. Then I saw that his name was Charles because it was on a patch sewn on to his dark blue shirt. He had slicked-back black hair and long sideburns. Rat would have called him a Greaser. I started to ask if Mrs. Worthington was home because I needed to collect for the paper but I decided the fewer words the better knowing how my luck was going and being that my lip was still a little puffy. I held out the newspaper for him.

He looked at me funny but opened the screen door and took the paper. His hands weren't exactly dirty but they looked like my hands after I had put a chain on my bike and then tried to scrub the oil off with washing powder.

Thanks. Uh. I'm Faye's cousin. Just helping out with a few things.

He closed the door while he was still looking me over.

If that Greaser Charles was Mrs. Worthington's cousin then I was a monkey's uncle. When grown-ups lie to kids they don't even try very hard. They think we're too dumb to know the difference. I didn't care who he was or what he was doing there. Then I thought about it more and decided that maybe I did care.

The only thing good that came out of me ringing that doorbell was learning that Mrs. Worthington's first name was Faye. That was a good name for me. That would be a Half-and-Half Word meaning I could probably say Faye about half the time without stuttering. Of course I could never call her Faye to her face but it was a good name in my book just the same.

I finished the route early and didn't know what I was going to do the rest of the afternoon when I saw Ara T pushing his cart across Melrose into the alley between Harbert and Peabody.

Mam liked to say that Ara T only had two speeds. Slow and slower. The cart jangled and rattled as he made his way to a bunch of garbage cans. The more the cart rattled the more the neighborhood dogs barked.

A second good idea for the day came to me.

Ara T would have to knock off from his junk collecting sometime and I could follow him at least until it got dark and maybe get to see where he kept his cart. He had to keep it somewhere at night. If he wasn't going to give me back my knife then I might be able to come up with a way to take it when he wasn't around.

The first thing I had to do was stash the yellow raincoat that made me stand out like one of those crossing guards at school. It wasn't raining and the raincoat was too hot anyway. I stuffed the yellow coat and one newspaper bag into my second bag.

I remembered the thick privet hedges around Mrs. Worthington's porch. That would be a good place to hide my bag. I could never get Rat to call them anything but Private Hedges even though I spelled out Privet for him. He told me not to be always worrying so much about words. But I did.

I went back to Mrs. Worthington's and pushed the bag under the hedges snug up to the porch. I sat behind the privet next to the porch which gave Ara T time to get up the alley a little ways. Being close to Mrs. Worthington's porch made me feel special like somehow I belonged there.

Following Ara T wasn't going to be easy because he was always looking up and back and to both sides when he was collecting junk. Ara T had a steady routine. He would push his cart up to a bunch of cans behind a house and take off all the lids first thing. He would then start picking through one can and put junk from that can in another one that didn't have as much in it. He would go through all the cans one at a time like that. I'll say this. He was neat. He put whatever he wanted in his cart then put the lids back on all the cans like he had found them. He didn't throw stuff around like you would think a junkman would do. Anytime he found a whiskey bottle he would hold it up and shake it. If it had even a little whiskey left in it he would put the bottle in a wooden crate in the back of his cart.

I let Ara T get about a dozen houses ahead of me and then I started creeping down the alley behind him.

Rat sometimes made me watch a detective show on television where this guy with a moustache named Boston Blackie would follow people around but they never saw him even though he was creeping only a few steps behind them in leather street shoes. Not even tennis shoes. Even a kid has enough brains to know that you can't follow somebody like that without them seeing or hearing you. I knew I was going to have to be careful following Ara T.

Every time Ara T would push his cart up to a bunch of cans I ducked behind a fence or into a garage that opened out to the alley. He looked back down my way a few times but I made sure he didn't see me. This went on for a long while. The muscles in my legs started hurting from scrunching behind so many cans.

Ara T didn't miss one can. Other than whiskey bottles he collected a few old shirts and a pair of old brown dress shoes and something that looked like an old toaster with a long cord. He also picked through magazines when he found a stack and put a few in his cart. He managed to grab the head of a wet mop that was hanging over a high fence and then hid the mop under the canvas tarp in his cart.

It was getting late and almost time to head back to Mrs. Worthington's to get my newspaper bags when Ara T stopped in back of a big three-story house that faced on Peabody. In the back of the house was a garage and some smaller buildings connected by a solid wooden fence that was taller than the other fences.

Ara T reached down to the bottom of the fence and pulled something out sideways that looked like a big nail. He did the same thing at the top of the fence. He then reached in his cart and got out what looked like an old car antenna. He stuck the antenna into a small hole in the fence and jiggled it. A big door screeched open. He took the handles of his cart and backed into the opening. The cart looked like it barely fit but then the door creaked to a close.

Without a handle or a knob the door looked like it was part of a plain fence. When I eased up closer I saw that it was probably the door to an old coal shed. I had found where Ara T kept his stuff.

My newspaper bags and raincoat were where I had left them under the hedges at Mrs. Worthington's house. I crawled up to the porch to get the bags and that was when I heard the sobbing.

I knew it was Mrs. Worthington because I also heard the ice in her glass clinking. She wasn't very far from me on the porch swing but it didn't sound like she was swinging. She was crying like when a girl falls off a playground ride and she isn't really hurt but just keeps on sobbing under her breath.

There was no way I could prove it but I knew Mrs. Worthington was crying on account of Greaser Charles.

I couldn't make myself leave Mrs. Worthington even though I couldn't figure out anything to do to help her. My legs were cramping again from squatting under the hedges. About the time I was getting ready to crawl out and head home a glass crashed on the concrete floor of the porch. I thought I would hear Mrs. Worthington get up from the swing but I didn't hear her moving.

I waited longer and listened harder. After a while lights started coming on at houses on both sides of Harbert. I pushed my newspaper bags from under the hedges with my feet and crawled out thinking I should just head on home but instead I gathered up my bags and eased around the corner of the porch. The blue Ford was gone. I climbed the steps.

Mrs. Worthington was lying on the swing with her head resting on one arm stretched straight out. She was wearing her green housecoat. Same as the first time I had seen her. I could smell the whiskey from the broken glass. She didn't have on shoes and she wouldn't be able to stand up without cutting her feet so I squatted down and started picking up the bigger pieces of glass one at a time. After putting them in a little pile beside the front door I brushed away the glass slivers with my newspaper bags.

Mrs. Worthington didn't move.

The other times I had looked at Mrs. Worthington it was her eyes and mouth mostly that I paid attention to but now I could see her skin was about as white as skin could get. As white as a new baseball right out of the box.

Talking is hard for me but listening and looking when you know things aren't the way they should be can be hard on me too.

I wanted Mrs. Worthington to get up from the swing and talk to me. Even ask me a question as long as it wasn't what my name was. I wanted to know why she was crying and if Greaser Charles had been mean to her. I wanted to see her pretty mouth move even if she didn't have on her red lipstick. I wanted to see her eyes looking at me again like she was glad I was standing in front of her. I wanted her to try to close the flaps of her housecoat. I looked at her until my neck started tightening up on me from being in one spot for too long and then I picked up my newspaper bags and shook out the glass slivers over the railing of the porch.

Mrs. Worthington squirmed a little and then moaned but she didn't wake up.

The first part of the way home I walked with my bags under my arm and then I took off running. I ran from lamppost to lamppost without stopping like I was running the bases. I touched each concrete post with my hand. I had always liked the big posts with the big glass globes sitting on top like a tall hat but when I wasn't feeling right inside the lampposts were like first basemen trying to tag me out.

At the last lamppost before I got to my house I made sure I stopped to catch my breath.

After I brushed my teeth I went to my parents' bedroom to tell them good night but my mother was at her dresser talking on the telephone to one of her friends about New Orleans. She blew me a good-night kiss. I went to find my father but he was in his office downstairs talking on the phone that he only used when he wanted to talk to people about what they should do with their money. No one in the house was supposed to answer my father's office phone except him and that was okay with me. My mother always said that I would as soon pick up a snake as a telephone and she was right about that. The only newspaper comic I didn't like was *Dick Tracy* because he talked on that phone on his wrist all the time.

Mam came into my room to pick up clothes and towels and tuck me in. She asked me why I had been so quiet after supper and I told her I was just thinking about the paper route and how I could change it up so I could finish it quicker each day. She didn't much like my answer. I can't lie very well when there are a lot of words to say or things to explain.

If I could have told her the truth I would have said that my mind was bouncing back and forth between Mrs. Worthington and Greaser Charles and Ara T and Mr. Spiro the way the pinball in the machine at Wiles Drug Store bounces off all the different colored lights. The pinball wouldn't stop.

Chapter Five

On Friday morning during the second week of my route I pitched the first inning in a practice game and then the coach told me he was taking me out because he wanted our team to get some fielding practice and that wouldn't happen if I was on the mound for the whole game.

When the coach said things like that it made me feel like I was a somebody instead of just a kid who couldn't talk right.

A guy I had nicknamed Racer had taken Rat's place as my catcher. He had to stick one of his mother's washrags inside his mitt so my hard throws wouldn't hurt his hand. Racer came over to me in the dugout.

You don't need to be throwing so hard in a practice game.

s-s-s-s-Only way I s-s-s-s-know how.

And why do you call me Racer?

I had to come up with something quick.

s-s-s-s-'Cause you run s-s-s-s-bases so fast.

Racer looked at me funny because he was one of the slowest guys on the team but at least it gave him something to think about besides talking to me.

I missed Rat every time I had to talk to somebody who didn't know me but it didn't do any good to think about Rat because I would just miss him more.

I had trouble cutting the cord again on the newspaper bundles that afternoon. It had been almost a week and Ara T still hadn't given my knife back. I had seen him from far away on the streets a few times and I knew he had seen me. I didn't know if he was avoiding me or I was avoiding him.

On that second Friday night of collections the envelope was clothes-pinned on the screen door at 1219 Vinton like it was supposed to be.

Through the screen I could tell that TV Boy was in his usual place in front of the television without the sound on. I took the envelope and counted the change. I marked the collection book and pinned the empty envelope back on the screen door. TV Boy was watching one of those stupid game shows where they asked questions that you would only know the answers to if you read encyclopedias all the time.

You sure wouldn't catch me near a show like that because if I was lucky enough to know the answer I wouldn't be able to get it out before the buzzer sounded. Buzzers and timers and watches made me nervous.

I was riding my bike for collecting because I wanted to get to Mr. Spiro's house early in case he had extra time to talk to me about the piece of the dollar bill he had given me. I pedaled up to his porch and pushed the kickstand down and went to ring the doorbell. Before I could get to the door it opened and there was Mr. Spiro with a book in his hand and a smile like he was glad to see me. His glasses were so far down on his nose that they didn't hook behind his ears.

Good evening, News Messenger. Is that fastball of yours giving the Heater from Van Meter a run for his money yet?

I knew he was talking about Bob Feller of the Cleveland Indians and I could have said a plain Yes and that would have been the end but I wanted to try to have a conversation with Mr. Spiro.

s-s-s-s-My favorite s-s-s-s-p

I started over so I could substitute the word *player* for *pitcher*. Even though both words were *P* words the *L* changed the way I made the first sound and that was all I needed sometimes to get started.

s-s-s-s-My favorite player is Ryne s-s-s-s-D

I promised myself not to pass out this time. I was careful to take a breath before trying to say Duren again. Just because Ryne Duren was my favorite baseball pitcher didn't mean I could say his name. Mr. Spiro was still smiling and looking straight at me.

s-s-s-s-D

No luck. The *D* sound stuck tight in my throat like a tennis ball in a chain-link fence. There wasn't any way to substitute a word.

If I say your player's full name do you think we might be able to say it in unison?

I nodded.

Mr. Spiro tilted his head back and rounded his lips and said Ryne Duren in a regular talking voice. The words came out of my mouth perfect at the same time they came out of his. Mam and Mr. Spiro were the only people who knew how to get me through a bad block and I had only known Mr. Spiro for a week.

Ah yes. The nearsighted Yankee reliever who makes batters tremble with his fastball.

How s-s-s-s-did you s-s-s-s-know to help me like that?

Mr. Spiro stepped down on the porch from his doorway.

Speech pathology is certainly not my field of expertise but it is an interesting subject that I've read a tad about of late. My guess is that you are also in control of your speech when you sing. Is that correct?

I nodded.

I'm glad you can share your song, Young Messenger. The pro-verbial bucket has not been constructed that would carry my piti-ful attempts.

Mr. Spiro put his hand in his pocket and brought out a handful of coins. He began counting out the ninety-five cents. I could feel words lining up in my head but it surprised me when they started to come out on their own without me doing a lot of planning and switching words ahead of time.

s-s-s-s-Would you have s-s-s-s-time to sit on the swing?

Certainly. I always have time for a Messenger of the News and this is porch-swinging weather if ever I've felt it.

Mr. Spiro went to the swing and sat on the side nearest the house. I sat down beside him and we started to swing. Easy.

I had another talking trick that worked almost the same as tossing a pencil in the air or saying the words at the same time somebody else did. Talking was easier for me in a swing if I got the timing right and pushed off at the same time I started to say a word. I did this with Mam some and she said I ought to practice swinging and talking more because it smoothed my words out but there usually weren't many swings handy when I needed to talk to somebody.

Mr. Spiro waited on me to start the conversation.

How did you s-s-s-s-know what happened to me last s-s-s-s-time . . . and why did you s-s-s-s-talk to me s-s-s-s-bout it?

The sentence was double the length I usually tried to get out but the words came easier on the swing. Mr. Spiro studied my question.

It occurred to me during what I assumed was a vocal block that you probably had encountered people who would not take the time to understand your situation. They would pretend to ignore it and that only leads to more confusion . . . for the speaker and the listener.

I liked the way Mr. Spiro didn't beat around the bush. Answering the question without any extra words and talking to me like I was a grown-up. He could have just said Lucky Guess but Mr. Spiro seemed like a guy who respected a kid enough not to lie or give a short answer.

I wanted to make certain you knew that your verbal blocks were of no bother to me. I'm interested more in content rather than how well one might vocalize it.

Most grown-ups and especially my relatives and friends of my parents treated me about as well as could be expected without them knowing exactly what I was going through when I tried to talk. Some people tried to finish sentences for me and mostly would get them wrong. Some people just smiled a fake smile and waited on me to get my words out while they were looking around the room. Some got confused and just wandered off as quickly as they could.

I knew that people didn't mean anything by it. If the way I talked was confusing for me it was bound to be confusing listening to me. But not one time had a grown-up except for Mam and my speech teacher talked to me about my stuttering. It's like I walked into a room with an organ-grinder's monkey sitting on my head and everyone pretending the monkey wasn't there. I barely knew Mr. Spiro but we were on his front porch having a talk about my stuttering.

I assume you are in the hands of a capable speech pathologist?

I nodded.

Do you think it's helping? Are you doing all that this person asks of you?

s-s-s-s-Most of the s-s-s-s-time.

From what I can understand, modern speech therapy is based on the Aristotelian logic that nonfluent speech is a product of improperly learned motor skills and has nothing to do with Freudian bugaboos.

Usually I could make out the meaning of what somebody said even if I didn't understand all the words but Mr. Spiro could tell he had lost me.

Putting it simply. Listen to your speech teacher. Practice what is taught and you will find your voice. It may not be the voice of your choosing but you will do well by it.

That was the first time anybody had ever told me that I had a fighting chance. Even my teacher. The day I first met her I asked how long it would take for her to teach me to talk like a regular kid and she said just to do my exercises and not worry about the future. How could I not worry about my future if I was going to be stuttering all the time in it?

I wanted to hear more from Mr. Spiro. His answers made me feel better no matter what my question was.

Why s-s-s-s-can most kids talk without any s-s-s-s-trouble and not s-s-s-s-me?

It was a simple question I had wanted to ask someone for as long as I could remember. Someone who would tell me the truth. I did ask

Mam one time but she said it was just God's plan. That didn't make any sense to me because a god who would play dirty tricks on a kid like that didn't know very much about being a god.

Mr. Spiro changed his smile. He had different smiles for different parts of a conversation.

I will play Socrates and ask you a question. Why can't everyone in the sixth grade throw a ball as hard and as straight as you can?

s-s-s-s-Because . . .

I didn't have a good answer. I didn't have any answer. He kept looking at me and waiting like I was going to have to come up with something before he would let me ask another question.

s-s-s-s-Because . . . they're not me.

Exactly, Messenger. So it follows that you are not them. Correct?

I nodded.

Your questions are filling our sails. We are making grand headway. Another one, if you will.

Why do s-s-s-s-people who can talk right waste so s-s-s-s-many words saying s-s-s-s-nothing?

Mr. Spiro smiled again. I was proud of my question because I thought it was one that he could really haul off and take a poke at.

Perchance do you know the name Voltaire?

I hadn't heard of the name but it started with the same sound as my name and so I didn't care much for it. I shook my head.

Voltaire was a French philosopher of two centuries past. He answered your question quite well. *La parole a eté donnée a l'homme pour déguiser sa pensée.*

Mr. Spiro moved his mouth the same as always but what came out was strange and exciting like if you turned on the kitchen faucet to get a drink of water and sweet lemonade came out instead.

Mr. Spiro smiled another new kind of smile.

Tis rude of me to go out of country but it's a favorite quote of mine that rings more true in the original French. It translates: Speech was given to man to disguise his thoughts.

I burned that sentence on to my brain like Ted Williams's name was burned on to my Louisville Slugger baseball bat.

I was the one smiling now. Whoever this Voltaire guy was he threw a hard one right down the middle when he said that. I guess people were using words to keep you from knowing what they were thinking when Mr. Voltaire lived in France and they were sure doing it big time in Memphis in 1959.

So many questions started whirling around in my head that I didn't know which one to pick. The question that came out didn't make any sense and I couldn't finish it because I didn't know what I was trying to ask.

Who s-s-s-s-thought up the letters and sounds that s-s-s-s . . . ?

My Gentle Air faded into thin air. Mr. Spiro looked at me until he knew my brain had completely stopped working.

If I understand your question, I believe you have Napoleon Bonaparte to blame.

s-s-s-s-The short s-s-s-s-guy?

A good laugh from Mr. Spiro.

While the short guy, as you refer to him, didn't invent the modern alphabet, he did help us preserve it.

I waited without saying anything because Mr. Spiro wasn't blinking and I knew he was getting ready to tell a good story.

Almost two hundred years ago our diminutive Napoleon was out and about doing his conquering in Egypt when one of his lieutenants brought him a large stone with writing on it. His army had found it near a town named Rosetta. They deduced the stone to be centuries old. When the British defeated Napoleon they took the Rosetta Stone to London. Archaeologists studied the writing and decided that our modern alphabet and the corresponding sounds actually came from Egyptian hieroglyphics.

Mr. Spiro could put so much information into his sentences that it hurt my head trying to keep up.

Hieroglyphics is tantamount to writing with pictures.

I remembered seeing the word *hieroglyphics* in *My Weekly Reader* but I had never heard it said out loud.

s-s-s-s-But words and letters can't be s-s-s-s-pictures.

He came back with questions that sent my mind off to the races.

Does *W* remind you of waves of water? Does a capital *H* remind you of the columns of a house? Does an *O* resemble the face of an owl? Does an *S* look like a snake?

I juggled the letters and waves and owls and snakes around in my head. How come nobody had ever told me that letters were more than sounds you made?

Mr. Spiro got to his feet. He took his glasses from the tip of his nose and slid them on top of his head.

Memory serves that I owe you the second installment of the incentive compensation I promised last week.

He reached inside the door and handed me another piece of a dollar bill. It was the lower left-hand corner. On it was written the word *servant* in the same careful hand that *student* had been written in the week before.

You now have one half of your golden fleece.

With Egyptian hieroglyphs and *My Weekly Reader* pictures of Cleopatra and snakes crawling around in my head I knew I was going to have trouble saying much more. When I got excited about something my talking went all the way haywire. I started thinking about what I was going to say three sentences ahead and then I got stuck on the sentence I was trying to get out. Words stirred around in my brain like the propeller on the milk shake machine at the drugstore.

I s-s-s-s-know about Jason and the s-s-s-s-A . . . and his gang.

There had been a story in *My Weekly Reader* called "The Golden Fleece" about Jason and the Argonauts who lived a long time ago trying to find a sheep with its wool made out of gold.

Good for you, Young Messenger.

s-s-s-s-Can I ask . . . was s-s-s-s-Jason real?

If you are asking if the story of Jason and the Argonauts is fiction or nonfiction, I will answer that there is no difference between the two in the world I inhabit. Therefore the question does not have a valid answer.

I felt like I was falling off a cliff and trying to grab for tree limbs or anything to slow me down like cowboys do in television shows.

s-s-s-s-But fiction is a story and s-s-s-s-nonfiction is the s-s-s-s-truth.

And I reply that you are referring merely to the rule of law. I contend that one is likely to find more truth in fiction. A good painting after all is more truthful than a photograph. Remember that, Young Messenger, for all your days.

I kept his words rolling around in my head until I was sure I had everything put away in the right place.

We'll have plenty of time to explore your queries at a later date but let's drop our sails for now.

One s-s-s-s-more question s-s-s-s-today. Do you s-s-s-s-know about s-s-s-s-Demosthe-s-s-s-s-nes?

I had wanted to say that name out loud ever since I had read in *My Weekly Reader* about this guy who lived a long time ago and had to put pebbles in his mouth to keep from stuttering.

Mr. Spiro smiled another kind of smile and then his head went back and he laughed a real honest-to-goodness laugh for the first time. It was a loud laugh. Almost like one of Mam's field whoops that she used to call me from my room.

Yes. But I suggest you not try putting pebbles in your mouth. You might accidentally swallow one.

Too late I wanted to tell him. I had already swallowed two of my shootin' marbles trying to copy Demosthenes. It might have worked a long time ago but not anymore. At least not with shootin' marbles.

Mr. Spiro started back into his house.

Thanks for your excellent service and good conversation, my young Candide. We have a date next Friday when we will continue to cultivate our garden.

He closed the door.

I had just finished the first official conversation I had ever had with a grown-up stranger. But Mr. Spiro didn't feel like a stranger to me anymore. He had said things that would keep me busy thinking all week and then I could come back for more next Friday.

Mr. Spiro had talked about his world. I wanted to know more about what was in it because he knew so much about my world. Bob Feller and Ryne Duren and Mr. Candide.

I needed to remember to ask Mr. Spiro who the Candide guy pitched for.

Chapter Six

I was anxious to get to Mrs. Worthington's house to see if my good luck would hold out. I couldn't beat two conversations in a single day with two strangers that I liked.

I pulled up on my bike at Mrs. Worthington's house right on time. I would be able to get the collections over to Rat's house before dark.

Mr. Worthington's black car was in the driveway and not the blue Ford that belonged to Greaser Charles. A good thing. I leaned my bike on the edge of the porch and ran up the steps. I heard shouting but I rang the bell anyway. The door jerked open. Mr. Worthington in a long-sleeved white shirt and blue necktie was sweating and red in the face like he had been doing push-ups in PE class.

Whaddya want?

The question surprised me along with the way he said it but I wasn't going to let anything twist me around. I had a trick I had been saving. Instead of trying to say *paperboy* I would use the second name of the newspaper that started with a good sound.

Scimitar.

I liked that word. There was a picture in my dictionary showing the scimitar to be a mean-looking curved sword. When I said the word the air came out of my mouth like the sound a sword would make if you sliced the wind with it.

Come back next week.

He started to close the door.

You owe s-s-s-s-two weeks.

The words came out of my mouth not sounding like my words because it was the first time I ever came close to talking back to a grown-up. And I didn't even stutter much. My right hand was opening and closing trying to find my scimitar again.

I told you to get lost, kid. I mean it.

The glass in the door rattled when he slammed it.

I didn't see this coming. I had never talked much to Mr. Worthington but I had seen him around and he had always seemed a nice enough guy. He cut his own yard with one of those push mowers that Ara T charged two dollars to sharpen. I got out the collection book to put a zero for the second time for 1396 Harbert when I heard glass breaking in the house. Then more yelling. It was Mr. Worthington.

Get your drunk ass up to the bathtub.

I'm not drunk . . . I'm shick of looking at you.

70

The voice was Mrs. Worthington's with her whiskey talking.

Every day I come home you're sot drunk. I'm tired of—

Mrs. Worthington interrupted Mr. Worthington by yelling louder than he was yelling.

You never come home when I need you. How . . . ?

Then something else crashed in the house that sounded like a piece of furniture being smashed. More glass broke and I could hear things rolling around on hardwood floors. More yelling. I backed off the porch and straddled my bike and headed for Rat's house. Lickety-split.

Mrs. Worthington was in trouble again like that time on the swing but I didn't have the first clue how to help her. Part of me wanted to go back and ring the doorbell again with my make-believe sword but the stuttering part of me said to ride away. That was the part I usually listened to.

I wished Rat were around to talk about what to do. Rat liked to say that two heads were better than one.

The best I could do was get away from Mrs. Worthington's as fast as I could. Running away is what I should call it. I pedaled my bike as fast as I could down Harbert. I turned the corner at Melrose and made a car swerve away from me. The driver honked the horn but I didn't look back. I pedaled until my sides hurt and there was no more air left inside of me.

Rat's mother came to the door.

How did collecting go tonight?

s-s-s-s-Fine . . . s-s-s-s-not fine.

Rat's mother looked at me like she was going to ask another question but she had been around me enough to know to let some of my words fall without picking them up. She knew she would need to do most of the talking.

We talked to Art last night. He's having a good time at his grandparents' and he's glad you're taking such good care of his route for him.

I didn't want to talk to Rat's mother about the route and especially didn't want to talk about what a good time Rat was having. He wasn't here and I was left to sort out a bunch of new feelings by myself. Ara T. Mrs. Worthington. Mr. Spiro. All were taking over my world in their own way. A world that Rat wasn't a part of because he was living it up on the farm. I gave Rat's mother the money I had collected.

s-s-s-s-Glad he's having a s-s-s-s-good time. See you s-s-s-s-n. . . .

I didn't feel like trying to finish my sentence because I was disguising what I really wanted to say like Mr. Voltaire had talked about. Rat's mother helped me out by smiling and closing the door.

When I turned onto my block I saw both of my parents' cars in the driveway and remembered that my mother had said they weren't going out Friday night and that the three of us were going to have a late supper at home.

I got off my bike and walked it to the garage. As I eased up the stairs I could hear Mam singing. She sang church songs mostly when there was someone around but I had heard her sing what she called Rounds when she thought she was by herself. I sat down at the top of the stairs to listen. ·

I went downtown to get my grip
I came back home just a pullin' the skiff
Just a pullin' the skiff
I went upstairs to make my bed
I made a mistake and I bumped my head
Just a pullin' the skiff
Just a pullin' the skiff
I went downstairs to milk my cow
I made a mistake and I milked that sow
Just a pullin' the skiff
Just a pullin' the skiff
Tomorrow tomorrow
Tomorrow never comes
Tomorrow tomorrow
Tomorrow's in the barn.

At least Mam was happy enough to sing. I knocked my special knock.

Get on back to the house, Little Man. You know yo' mammy and pappy's home. I fried you some chicken for dinner and they's waiting.

I didn't feel like trying to say anything. I knocked again. She opened the door.

All right. Get in here quick and tell me about paper collectin'.

Mam had a pile of my father's new white shirts by her chair. She had been cutting off the top buttons and sewing them back on by putting a little fork in between the button and the shirt. My father paid her extra to do this to all his new shirts because it made them easier to button at the neck. He said nobody could sew on a button like Mam. Not only could she sew better than anybody but she could do it with either hand. She also could iron clothes the same way.

I didn't know exactly what I wanted to beat around the bush about other than to ask Mam about Mrs. Worthington but I knew she wouldn't stand for talking about other people's business.

What do s-s-s-s-people feel like when they're s-s-s-s-drunk?

Mam stuck her needle and thread in the sleeve of the old checkered shirt she wore over her uniform. She gave me a hard look.

Law me. Why you askin' such a question?

It wasn't the kind of conversation Mam liked.

s-s-s-s-Just want to s-s-s-s-know.

I can't tell you what they feel but I know it puts the devil inside

74

'em and I know it never did nobody no good. Who you know that gets drunk?

s-s-s-s-Nobody . . . I see Ara T s-s-s-s-going through all those s-s-s-s-bottles like he's searching for a s-s-s-s-prize.

I had made the mistake of bringing up Ara T.

How many times do I have to tell you to keeps away from that man? He ain't found no prize and never will. He has the devil full inside him. We're not talkin' about such stuff no more.

I decided it was time to tell Mam that Ara T had my yellow-handle knife. I knew she would be upset but I hated to lie to Mam more than I hated her being mad at me. I knew I would have trouble getting all the words out.

s-s-s-s-I should have s-s-s-s-told you s-s-s-s-I gave my s-s-s-s-knife to Ara T to sharpen and he s-s-s-s-won't give it s-s-s-s-back. s-s-s-s-Sorry.

I was expecting Mam's mad look but she just got out of her chair and went to her chest of drawers. She looked in the cracked mirror above the chest with her quiet look. She put her little sewing fork in the top drawer and then sat down in her chair. She pulled her Bible onto her lap.

Don't be worryin' 'bout your jackknife. Get on to the house now and eat your fried chicken.

I went to the door. I wished Mam would get mad and say something mean but she knew that showing me how disappointed she was hurt me more than any words she could say.

s-s-s-s-Night, Mam.

Good night, Little Man.

At the supper table I had one piece of chicken and then I asked my parents to be excused. My mother reached over and put her hand on my forehead.

Are you feeling okay? You seem a little hot.

s-s-s-s-I'm fine. s-s-s-s-Tired.

My father wiped his mouth with his napkin.

Is everything working out on the paper route?

Okay. s-s-s-s-But I'll s-s-s-s-be glad when Rat's s-s-s-s-back.

I bet you will, son. I know you miss having him around. Anything you want to talk about?

I shook my head. Part of me was wanting to tell my father about my knife and how Ara T was acting and that I had made Mam upset but it was all so jumbled up in my head that there was no way I could start picking through that many words.

In my room I took out Rat's collection book where I had put the second piece of the dollar from Mr. Spiro. Then I took my billfold out of the desk drawer. The two pieces—*student* and *servant*—were from the same bill because they matched up exactly when I put them together. I tucked them both in my billfold behind my Ryne Duren baseball card.

Mr. Spiro had something in mind besides just a money tip when he started giving me the pieces of a dollar with the words. I couldn't figure out what the two words had to do with each other but Rat would be home in two weeks and I would have all four pieces of the puzzle by then. I thought about us working on the puzzle together and how much fun that would be.

Going to sleep would have been hard if I started thinking about Rat and all the great dirt-clod fights he was having on the farm with his cousins. I got the pillow from the other twin bed and put it on top of me and put my arms around it. Whenever I started feeling all alone it felt good to have something to hang on to.

Chapter Seven

Mrs. Worthington was sitting on her porch swing on Monday of my third week on the route.

I had been hoping for a grown-up conversation with her like the one I had had with Mr. Spiro but she just gave me a plain old Thank-you when I walked up on her porch to hand her the paper.

She did have a smile for me. A sad one. She didn't act like she was drinking whiskey but I got the feeling she had gobs of stuff on her mind. She looked straight ahead like when your eyes really don't see anything because your brain is thinking hard about something else.

Cool for July.

I had practiced those three words over and over on the way to her house in case I might see her. My air was so gentle you couldn't hear it. Mrs. Worthington turned halfway to look at me and nodded. I waited for her to say something but there wasn't anything else coming from her and all my practiced words with easy starting sounds were used up. Mrs. Worthington spoke to me after I started back down the steps.

Do I owe for the paper?

She owed two weeks which I figured in my head was a dollar and ninety cents but I didn't want to take a chance on an *N* sound. On Friday the amount would be two dollars and eighty-five cents which might be easier for me to say.

Wait till Friday.

The *W* and *F* sounds let out their own air without me having to wrestle with them and the *T* sound came out in a whisper but I had spoken two complete sentences to Mrs. Worthington without stuttering. I hoped she could tell how hard I was working on my talking for her.

She went inside her house and closed the door that Mr. Worthington had almost busted the glass out of the week before. Mrs. Worthington didn't have to say much for me to tell what kind of day she was having. I had already seen her angry eyes. Her happy eyes. Her whiskey eyes. I had just seen her empty eyes.

Mrs. Worthington's eyes stayed in my head all the way home and that should have been a warning to me that things were going to be bad for the rest of the day.

When I came downstairs from getting cleaned up my mother told me that Mam had asked for the evening off but the worst news was that we were going out to eat at a sit-down restaurant.

I only liked to eat out at cafeterias where you could point to what you wanted but we headed to a fancy Italian restaurant downtown.

The night kept getting worse. My parents ran into some loud-talking people they knew at the restaurant and asked them to join us. Eight grown-ups including my parents ended up at our table which was eight too many grown-ups for me since I was the only kid there.

My mother put her hand on my crew cut and rubbed it like she was trying to wipe something out of my hair.
　　Our big boy will be twelve soon.

The women clapped and oohed and aahed and one of the men put his hand on my shoulder.
　　I hear this boy has quite an arm on him. Let's feel that muscle.

He put his hand around my upper arm.
　　Yep. Feels solid to me.

I wanted to tell him that big muscles didn't have anything to do with throwing. That it was the way a person used the muscles that he had. But there was no way I could ever figure out a way to say all those words without using tons of Gentle Air.

The grown-ups drank wine from fat bottles wrapped in little ropes and talked about business and houses and other stuff that didn't mean anything and they laughed at what the other one said even though it wasn't funny. They left me alone eating little sticks of hard bread and drinking lemonade that was sour because all the sugar was caked in the bottom. I knew with my parents talking to their friends there was a good chance that they would forget to order for me. I couldn't stop worrying about it as the waiter went around the table in his white coat with a towel on his arm.

I decided that since my parents were making me eat with all the grown-ups I was going to order something I liked no matter what. Spaghetti.

The S sound would be easy enough for starters but the P sound that backed it up would give me a problem for sure. Just before the waiter got to me I figured out how I could change Spaghetti to make it come out of my mouth easier. That was a trick I used sometimes when I only had to say one word and when I could feel the word getting stuck in my throat ahead of time. The word would only have to be changed a little to make it come out and that was better than tossing a knife or fork in the air to start my word because somebody could get hurt if I did that.

It was my turn. The waiter stood over me with his pencil and pad.
    And what for you, young man?
    Shplishghetti.

The word had seemed okay when I was going over the sound changes in my head but it sounded first-grade stupid when I said it out loud.

The waiter smiled like I had told some kind of a joke. The woman at the table sitting next to my mother laughed. Her husband had been lighting cigarettes for her all night like she was too dumb to know how to use a Zippo. When she blew smoke out of her mouth she would lift her head and blow it up in the air like she was proud of herself.

Your son is such a daw-w-w-w-ling.

The woman put extra Ws in the word like she was trying to make it up to my parents for laughing at me.

My face felt hot with everybody staring at me like I was Clarabell the Clown on a stage without a horn to honk. The burning in my face and neck wouldn't go away. The grown-ups finally stopped looking at me and started talking and smoking and drinking their wine like everything would be hunky-dory if they just ignored me.

I didn't feel like eating when the waiter put the plate of spaghetti in front of me but I figured there wasn't anything else to do. My face was still burning and I was hoping the spaghetti might calm me down.

The spaghetti didn't taste good when I put it in my mouth but I kept eating it just so I would have something to do. I started eating more bread sticks and drinking the sour lemonade to get rid of the bad spaghetti taste but it just got worse.

Spaghetti. Wine. Cigarette smoke. Zippo fumes. Perfume. All the smells in the restaurant started to glom together inside my nose. I got dizzy like the night on Mr. Spiro's porch. The spaghetti wasn't going to stay down for much longer and there wasn't anything I could do to stop it. My eyes felt it coming.

My mother looked at me like I should do something quick but my mouth jerked open before I could grab the red cloth napkin in my lap. Spaghetti and everything else inside me—the whole shootin' match as Rat liked to say—was set free with an air that wasn't the least bit gentle. I let go all over the table.

My parents and their friends jumped up to try to get out of the path of the flying spaghetti. Waiters started running around with towels and mops and my mother began apologizing to everybody and saying they needed to get me home because I probably was Coming Down With Something.

The Something I Was Coming Down With was the same thing I had been coming down with every minute of my talking life.

My parents tried to have a conversation with me on the way home but I didn't have anything to say. They knew when to give up. I sat in the backseat and watched all the people on the streets of downtown Memphis. At the bus stops. At the train station. Sitting on porch steps. They were all talking. Talking up a storm. I couldn't get out one simple word without ruining everybody's night out.

When we got home I went upstairs to brush the bad taste out of my mouth and get in bed even though it was only eight o'clock. It was hard to get the restaurant out of my head and then I started feeling even worse that I had messed up supper for everybody. They hadn't done anything wrong. My parents and their friends should have been able to eat at a restaurant if they wanted to without getting spaghetti spewed all over them. Even the woman who laughed at me and didn't know how to use a Zippo.

I decided the right thing to do was to go downstairs and tell my parents I was sorry. I also needed to see if Mam had put anything in the icebox before she left because my stomach was growling and telling me it needed something in it where the big pile of spaghetti should have been.

My mother and father were talking in the breakfast room as I eased down the back stairs. I sat on the landing step to hear what my mother was saying.

His therapist said that stammering is likely generic but no one in my family stammers.

I think you mean *genetic*.

My father was all the time correcting my mother on her words. She would get close to the right one but close doesn't cut it when it comes to words. And she always had to say that the way I talked was Stammering. Maybe it sounded better to her than Stuttering.

My father spoke again.

I wish he wouldn't pretend that he doesn't have a stutter. He needs to realize it's not something he should be ashamed of.

Do you think his therapist knows what she's doing?

She came highly recommended from the school, didn't she? She seems . . .

I didn't want to hear any more talk about me.

When I tiptoed back up the stairs I knew I had heard something important but I couldn't figure out exactly what. I kept going over what my mother said about stammering not running in her family and that made me wonder if stuttering ran in my father's family. And why he didn't say anything about that.

My mother said I could have whatever I wanted when I came down for breakfast the next morning but I told her that cereal was fine. She asked me if my stomach was feeling better.

s-s-s-s-It's o-s-s-s-s-kay. Sorry for s-s-s-s-last s-s-s-s-night.

Don't worry. Everybody gets a bug now and then.

Stuttering is not a bug. AND I DIDN'T JUST COME DOWN WITH SOMETHING. I screamed the words inside my head but that was where they stayed.

I crunched my cereal as hard as I could so the sound would take the place of the talking in my head. My mother sipped her coffee and turned the pages of the morning newspaper.

They've announced the lineup for the Mid-South Fair. It'll be here before you know it. I guess you'll want to go this year again with Art.

I nodded.

I don't know if I approve of the aurora of the fair . . . I mean aroma . . . Oh I don't know what I mean.

I nodded.

She probably meant the Aura of the fair and I didn't have any problem with it. I liked to throw balls at the lead milk bottles because I could usually knock them over and get a prize. Rat and I would walk up and down the midway and try to figure out what was in all the sideshows. We stood in line last year to get into the hypnotist's tent. We were going to tell the Great Something or Other to put me under a spell so I could talk right and then Rat wouldn't let anybody clap their hands to snap me out of it. But we chickened out when it came time to go in because Rat said the guy might make a mistake and turn me into a barking dog.

After breakfast my mother said she had to go to one of her meetings at the country club and that I should stay in my room and read since Mam was still gone.

s-s-s-s-Where's Mam?

She called this morning to say she needed a little more time off. She deserves it, don't you think.

I nodded.

From the kitchen I watched my mother get in her car and back it down the driveway. She stopped at the street and reached into her handbag for a cigarette. She pushed in the lighter on the dashboard and rolled her window down. She put the lighter to her cigarette and then blew the smoke out the window.

My mother had told me at the beginning of the summer that she had stopped smoking and made me promise that I never would start. I knew she hadn't quit because I could smell it on her clothes. But I didn't care if she smoked or not. My father smoked and he never made any bones about it.

I headed upstairs.

When I passed my parents' bedroom I noticed that one of the doors to the big closet was open a few inches. Most closets in the house were small but my father had paid some men to knock a hole in the wall and turn the smaller bedroom next door into their closet. It was so big that it had two doors going into it. I was not allowed inside because that was where my father kept his shotguns for hunting. I felt creepy going in but I did anyway. I pushed the light switch on and closed the door.

I remembered once seeing my mother get out a big round hatbox she kept in the closet. It had a bunch of papers and pictures in it and I could tell by the way she handled them that they were special to her. I had been meaning to take a look inside the box ever since and I decided that the right time had come.

The first thing that hit me was the smell of mothballs. My mother put mothballs everywhere. In all the closets. In all the chest of drawers. In the attic. A moth would be committing suicide if it came near our house.

My father's suits were lined up on one side and my mother's dresses on the other. My father's guns were standing up in the corner in a long rack that had a lock on it. I saw the big hatbox on a high shelf. I piled some suitcases on top of one another and climbed up to get the box.

The first batch of papers I came to was all my report cards from the first grade on. Tied up with the report cards was a letter to my parents from the school principal with *Private* written on the envelope in red ink. I knew what was in the letter. It had to do with the time after the first grade that the principal said I was reading and writing like a third grader or even a fourth grader which meant the school would let me skip a grade but he didn't think I should because of the way I talked. My mother went to see the principal and told him with me sitting there that he had better not hold her son back because letting me skip a grade would show her friends that I was just as smart as their kids even though I couldn't talk right. Before I knew it I had been moved up to the third grade.

Next in the hatbox was a thick book with heavy black pages full of photographs. My father was in a bunch of the pictures. He was easy to pick out because he was so tall and thin and had blond hair.

I went through the rest of the papers and folders as fast as I could. Just a bunch of diplomas and newspaper clippings and other stuff with my father's name on them. At the very bottom of the box I came to a brown envelope without any writing on the outside.

Inside was a small piece of paper that said "Birth Certificate Of" and the name written in longhand was "Baby Boy." The date on it was my birthday. My mother's name before she got married was written in at the bottom of the paper on the left beside MOTHER. On the right side next to FATHER was a word I wasn't expecting.

Unknown.

I put everything away in the box like I had found it and went to my room to lie down on my bed and start some serious thinking.

When I heard my mother's car in the driveway and the car door close I slipped out of my hard thinking and ran to the big closet to make sure I had turned off the light and shut the doors.

Both closet doors stood open and the light was on which let me know I had been in there for sure and I wasn't just dreaming about what I had seen. I turned off the light and fixed the doors like I had found them and ran to the bathroom to run water in the tub. I didn't usually take a bath that early in the day but I decided I smelled too much like mothballs.

Chapter Eight

I probably get over things that hurt faster than most kids. I don't have much of a choice seeing as how my stuttering hurts me so many times during a day.

Rat has a big scar on his left arm from the time he crashed his bike trying to ride down the concrete steps at Crump Stadium. He tells anybody who listens about how the doctor had to sew sixteen stitches in his arm. He likes to show off to guys and make girls scream by sticking a safety pin in the scar. He says he can't feel the pin but I can tell he's careful not to push it in too far.

I used to have my own secret trick but I used a thumbtack instead of a safety pin. If I knew I was going to have to read or recite in class I would keep a thumbtack in my hand and push it into my palm when I started to talk. I kept hoping the pain would make me forget about stuttering but it never did. I decided it didn't make much sense to keep sticking myself and I got tired of always having a bloody hand when class was over. You can't replace one hurt with another one. You just end up with double hurts.

Walking the paper route each day gave me time to think about what I had found in the closet.

Here was the toughest part to figure out. If some other man and my mother got together to make me then why did I like being around my father more than my mother? I liked to talk to my father a whole lot more than I did my mother. My father never seemed to mind that I stuttered so much. He even said when I turned thirteen he would be buying me a shotgun and he wanted to take me hunting with him and his friends. I knew he was always tired when he got home from work and he really didn't like to pitch and catch much but he always took the time to do it if I asked him.

Finding out my father was Unknown answered one big question. I had always tried to figure out how I could have such a good arm on me when my father threw so soft. Almost like a girl. I had always wondered if I was going to be tall and thin like my father when I got older. I guess I knew the answer to that question unless the other man who made me was tall too. But I didn't have the first notion of who that man was or if he was short or tall.

I thought so much about what I had seen in the closet that week that I would come to the end of my route and look down in my newspaper bags and wonder where all the papers had gone. But I don't think I ever missed a house because I never got a complaint. My arms and legs could do things without my mind knowing about it.

Friday morning my father surprised me by saying he was going to take off work that afternoon and we could have lunch anywhere I wanted and then take in a matinee.

I told him I had to be at the paper drop by three o'clock and he said he would make sure I got there. We checked the paper and the only movie time that worked out was a western called *Shane* playing at the Crosstown Theatre. He said he saw the movie years ago when it first came to town but it was good enough to see again and he thought I would like it. He said for me to be ready at noon. We would eat at Britling's Cafeteria and then go to the movie.

At noon I was waiting on the back steps with my newspaper bags when my mother came outside to tell me that my father's secretary had called to say that he had gotten caught in a meeting and was running late. My mother said she would fix me a pimento cheese sandwich for lunch and then my father and I could go straight to the movie.

s-s-s-s-Could I have just s-s-s-s-cheese?

You can't have a pimento cheese sandwich without pimentos in it.

I wanted to tell my mother that Mam never put pimentos in my cheese because I thought the red specks looked like pieces of glass but sometimes it was easier to eat glass than explain things to my mother.

Mam wasn't at home to fix my lunch because she had called to tell my mother that she needed a little more time off. I couldn't remember the last time Mam had been gone more than one night. Something didn't feel right that she would be away for so long without me knowing where she was.

My father's Buick screeched into the driveway about the time I swallowed my last piece of glass. He motioned for me to jump in.

I'm sorry about lunch, son. The meeting was important.

I nodded.

I wanted you to have a nice lunch of your choosing. I know the dinner the other night wasn't much fun.

I nodded again. I thought about saying that eating glass wasn't too much fun either.

Your mother and I are proud of you for taking on Art's paper route. It shows how responsible you're becoming.

I nodded and then thought my father deserved more than a nod for what he had said.

s-s-s-s-Thanks.

When the movie was about half over I whispered to my father that Shane was going to ride into town and take care of the bad guys so that the mother and father and their boy could be safe on their farm even though Shane was in love with the boy's mother. I don't stutter as much when I whisper so I was able to say all that without much trouble. My father slapped me on the knee and whispered back.

How'd you know that?

94

I smiled at my father. Sometimes I could see endings to movies in my head like the beardy old man in Coldwater could see what was going to happen to Mam's brother.

When the lights in the theater came on my father said we had to hurry so I could start my route on time. I didn't say much when we got in the car because I was working on a question. It took a lot of planning ahead on the words.

s-s-s-s-Do you think the s-s-s-s-boy looked more like his s-s-s-s-father or like Shane?

I guess his father. Why?

s-s-s-s-Do boys always s-s-s-s-look like their fathers?

More often than not . . . but it's not always a given.

I was looking out the windshield but I felt my father glance over at me when he said it wasn't a Given. I thought about asking him if Shane could have been the boy's father because it was plain that Shane had an eye for the mother but then I started getting confused about what was in the movie and what was in the story in my head.

We got to the drop about the same time as the newspaper truck.

Made it right on time. Don't forget your bags in the back. I enjoyed the movie.

s-s-s-s-Me too. s-s-s-s-Thanks for s-s-s-s-taking off work.

Next time we eat out it will be at Britling's. I promise.

My father pulled his car out on Bellevue and headed back downtown toward his office.

I folded my papers in world-record time once I got the movie out of my head and the kid yelling Shane Shane Come Back Shane. I think that kid was lonesome like me but he was only in the movies and I was living my real stuttering life.

I noticed Big Sack sitting in his truck parked across the street and watching me. It was the second time during the week I had seen him just sitting like that which didn't seem right because he was usually mowing lawns or cleaning out flower beds.

Ara T hadn't been around all week but I spotted him a ways down the alley when I was lifting the bags off the fence onto my shoulders. The way he was sneaking looks at me made me wonder if Mam had gotten my knife back from him. One thing was for sure. Ara T was going through the garbage cans a new way. He would pull stuff out of a can and throw it anywhere. His neat way of collecting junk was gone.

I almost ran for the first part of my route. I was breathing hard by the time I got to Mr. Spiro's house. It wasn't time to collect but I had something special to talk to him about.

I had worked on a list of questions for Mr. Spiro all week in my room. I didn't want to forget anything important so I had typed the three questions on a clean piece of notebook paper.

1. Why do most grown-ups treat me like I'm not a real human being?

2. When does a kid become a grown-up?

3. What can I do to be smart like you?

That wasn't everything I wanted to talk about but that was all I could get out of my head and down on paper.

I didn't want to be out of breath if we had our talk so I sat down on the curb across the street and refolded some papers that weren't as tight as Dick's hatband. I asked my mother once who Dick was when she talked about his hatband but she never would tell me.

I noticed an old bicycle leaning against the side of Mr. Spiro's house. It had a basket on the front handlebar and a flat piece of wood on the back behind the seat. The handlebars and the spokes on the wheels were rusted but the chain looked like it was in good shape.

About the time my refolding was done Mr. Spiro came out of his door with a book under his arm and holding a thick white coffee mug that was steaming. I didn't see how anybody could be drinking hot coffee in the middle of the hottest part of the Memphis day but it seemed to suit Mr. Spiro. He waved me over when he saw me on the curb.

What news do you bring me today, Messenger?

I knew he meant newspaper news but it was my chance to see if we could have another long talk. I lifted the straps of the newspaper bags over my head and laid them on the porch.

s-s-s-s-Would you have s-s-s-s-time to s-s-s-s-answer some questions?

Certainly.

Mr. Spiro took a sip of his steaming coffee.

I have a good cup of joe and a good traveler at my side.

Anybody else would have answered with one or two words but Mr. Spiro made you feel like he was excited about the same thing you were excited about.

We sat on the porch swing. I reached into the back pocket of my shorts and pulled out the piece of paper with my questions. It was only a little wet from sweat. I handed it to Mr. Spiro. He didn't take it.

Our goal is dialogue, Messenger. That takes two. I have all the time we need so I would like to hear you ask your questions.

I should have known Mr. Spiro wouldn't let me get away with just handing him my list. I looked down at the piece of paper to start getting the first question lined up inside my head.

s-s-s-s-Do grown-ups think s-s-s-s-kids are humans?

Yes.

I waited because no eye blinks meant there was more coming.

That is the quick answer to your query but I believe the question you really wish to ask is: Are adults good at communicating with young people?

Mr. Spiro had hit the nail on the head. Then he answered the question.

I'm afraid I would have to answer that query in the negative.

Why?

I asked it without a stutter because Ws have built-in Gentle Air.

More reasons than we can know but I would sum up by saying it's because many adults are uncomfortable with themselves.

That answer took some going over in my head. Mr. Spiro gave me a few seconds and then went on.

Adults—or grown-ups as you most graciously refer to them—have a difficult time talking with children because young people don't understand the code.

Mr. Spiro twisted toward me on the swing.

Example. An adult says: I'll have to think about that. What do you think the adult means?

I shook my head even though my mother said that to me all the time.

The translation is: What you asked about is not going to happen so don't bring up the matter again.

I smiled because that was what it usually meant for me.

s-s-s-s-Tell me some s-s-s-s-more 'bout the s-s-s-s-code.

What do you think adults mean when they say: That's not something we should talk about until you're older?

I shook my head again.

It can be decoded as: I don't know how to answer you.

When will I be an s-s-s-s-adult?

Who's to say? You might be further along than you realize.

Mr. Spiro got up from the swing.

I am a rude host. I have this good cup of coffee and you are without sustenance. How would a lemonade suit you?

I wasn't all that thirsty because my father had bought me a giant Coca-Cola at the movie but Mr. Spiro was already headed into the house before I could get anything out of my mouth. He came out soon with a glass of lemonade about as big as I could hold in one hand. It was sweet like Mam made it because she always made sure the sugar was stirred up. The glass was full of big lemons that were cut in half and squeezed. Not like the thin slices my mother cut and that you couldn't do anything with. I took big swallows.

Now let me ask a few questions while you imbibe.

He asked me questions that I could answer mostly with a Yes or a No. The best kind of questions for me.

Do you like school?

s-s-s-s-Most times.

Do you have siblings?

s-s-s-s-No.

What does your father do for a living?

I thought about telling Mr. Spiro what I had seen on my birth certificate in the closet but decided the time wasn't right to talk about that.

s-s-s-s-He takes care of s-s-s-s-money for s-s-s-s-people.
Do you think he enjoys his work?

I nodded.
s-s-s-s-He spends s-s-s-s-plenty of time s-s-s-s-doing it.

Then Mr. Spiro said one of those things that seemed important without me knowing why.

One of the most beautiful happenstances of life is the person doing precisely what he knows is intended for him. Unfortunately a rare situation.

I let the words stay on the blackboard in my head.

I looked down at my wrinkled piece of paper for another question.

How s-s-s-s-can I be smart s-s-s-s-like you?

Mr. Spiro let out another one of his short laughs and then took a long drink of coffee. He looked straight ahead like he was working on the answer or making a plan.

Would you care to come inside for a moment?

I looked away and wasn't sure what to say. Rat had told me that going into a house on the route was against the rules. Mr. Spiro stood.

I know it might be against newspaper regulations or against your parents' wishes but I can assure you it is proper in this context.

I didn't have to think too long because I had wanted to see the inside of Mr. Spiro's house all along. I was nervous but not from knowing I might have to say something. The nervousness came from being excited just like before the first pitch of a ball game.

The house was not going to be like my house. I was sure of that. But I didn't know what to expect. Never in a gazillion years could I have guessed what I was going to see.

Books. Hundreds. Thousands. Wall to wall. Floor to ceiling.

But it wasn't like a library because the books weren't on shelves. They were in wooden crates with the crates laid on their sides and stacked on top of each other. The crates were different sizes and reminded me of giant alphabet blocks the way they were stacked on the floor. Some crates still had the bright-colored paper stickers on the side showing that the boxes had been used for oranges or bananas and some of the crates had words on them written in foreign languages.

In the living room the crates covered almost every part of the walls leaving openings only for doors and windows. A big stuffed chair sat in the middle of the room with a floor lamp next to it. On the left side of the room was a pair of glass-paned doors leading to another room that had even more crates of books. A small bed covered with a white sheet and a double-sized pillow with arms on it sat in the middle of the floor with books scattered around it. A ceiling light with an extra long cord hung down so that the lightbulb dangled just above the bed.

Mr. Spiro went somewhere in the back of the house and came out with a metal folding chair. He unfolded it with a pop and put it down facing it toward the big chair in the front room.

I don't receive many visitors so my accommodations are crude. But young bones like yours should not require cushions.

I walked over to the metal chair but couldn't make myself sit. I circled it and started walking around the room to see the books up close.

I finally sat down with my head still twisting on my shoulders. Mr. Spiro was in his chair but he wasn't saying anything. Like Mam he seemed to know when I was thinking too hard to be interrupted and he just let me twist in the chair for a while.

What's in the s-s-s-s-books?

With all the good questions I could have asked that was about the dumbest one I could have come up with.

All the world and more.

Even when I asked a bad question Mr. Spiro had a good answer for it.

But shall we get back to your prepared questions? I know they are important to you.

My sheet of paper was still in my hand but wadded up now like a popcorn sack at the end of a Memphis Chicks' game. I tried to smooth it and get my mind back on my questions.

Where s-s-s-s-do I start learning?

It wasn't the best question but it was as close as I could get to what I thought I wanted to ask.

Mr. Spiro was looking at me like when you're at bat and you look around at the third base coach for a sign and he's staring at you like he's trying to send you the words through the air.

You've already made good headway but let me warn you that the word *Start* implies that there is a Finish. That's something that we should discuss at some point.

I couldn't keep my head from twisting. I had never seen so many books outside of a library. I managed to come up with a question that made more sense than the last one.

Where s-s-s-s-did you s-s-s-s-get the s-s-s-s-books?

All over the world. At every port there are good books to be had for a pittance. Some merchant marines carve broom handles to pass the time at sea. I chose to spend my thirty years on the high seas reading and studying.

I knew about regular marines but not the merchant kind. Asking the question was going to be hard because two words in a row with the same starter sound usually did me in.

What are s-s-s-s-m . . . What are s-s-s-s-those kind of s-s-s-s-marines?

Merchant marines are men of peace and cargo. Distributing the world's goods. A vital service and a proper vocation for the curious mind and restless heart.

s-s-s-s-How did you s-s-s-s-get to s-s-s-s-Memphis?

I found my books fit nicely on a towboat captained by a good friend going upriver from New Orleans. When I saw the city sitting high on its bluff, I knew I had reached my new anchorage from which to explore North America. My homeport is where my books are.

I made myself focus on one crate of books at eye level in back of Mr. Spiro. Somebody named Heidegger had written all the books in the crate.

What is your compass locked in on, Messenger?

I got out of my chair and walked over to the crates and put my finger on a book. *Being and Time.*

Martin Heidegger. A German philosopher who is still very much with us. He helps us understand existentialism. Something you may want to look at later on in your voyage.

What is s-s-s-s-exist . . . ? s-s-s-s-That word s-s-s-s-you said.

Existentialism simply means a person exists as a being because that person alone gives meaning to his or her own life.

I had trouble getting my brain to hold on to that so Mr. Spiro kept on going for me.

A pity that Heidegger fell in with the Nazis. Remember, my young Messenger, that intelligence doesn't always equate to moral actions.

When most grown-ups talked about things you didn't know anything about it was like they were trying to let you know that they were smarter than you. But when Mr. Spiro told me about something new all I felt was that I just wanted to know more.

Heidegger was a top crate for many years but he has slipped somewhat. He is still a valuable companion if you can winnow the immoral chafe.

Mr. Spiro was trying to let me in on one of his secrets and I had a hunch what he might be talking about.

You s-s-s-s-move these s-s-s-s-crates around a lot.

Right you are, Messenger. Knowledge is not static. It has an ebb and flow much like the tides.

Are all these s-s-s-s-books about s-s-s-s-philosophy stuff?

Certainly not. Too much theory makes for a secondary existence. One should practice as well as preach.

Mr. Spiro got up from his chair and walked around the room and put his hand on different crates.

English fiction. Russian fiction. The Medievals. Shakespeare. Biographies. Politics. Science, both modern and classical. Geology. I find myself fascinated by the study of landmasses. No doubt because of so much time spent bobbing up and down at sea.

I got up and walked around the room from crate to crate. The books were old and worn and most had pieces of paper sticking out the top.

s-s-s-s-Do you have s-s-s-s-p . . . ?

Poetry was a word I always had trouble saying but I was going to blast it out of my mouth if that was what it took.

Do you have S-S-S-S-POETRY BOOKS?

I had to shout to make the words come out. Yelling was like whispering. They both made words more of a sure thing. I never yelled words in school but I sometimes did it around grown-ups if I knew they wouldn't think I was off my rocker.

You have so quickly discovered one of my many deficiencies. I once considered poetry a form of indulgent shorthand but I have worked to overcome my bias.

I wrote a s-s-s-s-p— I wrote one.

I couldn't believe what I was hearing coming out of my mouth. I had never told anyone that I had written a poem. Not even Mam or Rat. I had hidden the poem away in an encyclopedia volume after I had typed it.

Perhaps you will help me with my bias. Shall we hear your poem?

I knew I couldn't ask Mr. Spiro if I could write it for him. He wouldn't let me get away with that. I sat down in the chair thinking about the poem smashed flat on paper in the *P* volume of the encyclopedia at home. I could say the poem in my head but there was no use trying to say it out loud.

s-s-s-s-Can't say the words.

Shall we try reciting in unison?

It was worth a shot. I didn't stutter when my class recited the Pledge of Allegiance or when I said the twenty-third psalm with Mam.

I'll retrieve some paper. You transcribe your poem for me and we will recite together.

s-s-s-s-Do you have a s-s-s-s-typewriter?

Even better, Messenger. You are the modern communicator.

Mr. Spiro went into another room and came back with a gray case. He opened the snaps on each side and pulled out a typewriter. It was smaller than the one in my room. He put it on a table and brought the table over to where I was sitting. He gave me a clean sheet of white paper and I started typing. The typewriter keys didn't feel like my keys at home but the words started coming out on the paper just the same even though my hands were shaking a little.

I wish I had a book . . .

Mr. Spiro picked up a magazine and started reading while I typed. When I had finished I rolled out the sheet of paper and handed it to him. He pushed his glasses up from the tip of his nose and studied the poem as we sat in our chairs facing each other. He asked me with his eyes if I was ready. I watched his mouth and we started saying the poem together.

I wish I had a book
That did not have an end.
I go to pick it up
And it is new again.

The words feel real
And mine to share.
They have no sound.
They have no air.

My voice is clear
And lets me speak.
My fear is gone.
I'm never weak.

My words all come
And right on time.

The words are true
The words are mine.

The poem didn't sound like my words even though I had just typed them. Each word floated out of my mouth and joined up with Mr. Spiro's to make one. I didn't stutter once or have to worry about Gentle Air or sneaking up on sounds or fainting. My legs were itching. I looked down to see sweat trickling over my kneecaps and down my legs. For the first time I had said words out loud that I had written on paper.

Mr. Spiro was smiling with his big arms folded across his chest. He looked at me for a while without saying anything and then stood.

My bias against poetry has been properly challenged. A wonderful poem. I'm grateful to you for sharing, my Stuttering Poet.

If someone had called me a Stuttering Boy or a Stuttering Sixth Grader or a Stuttering Pitcher I would have probably tried to pick up something and bust them. But Stuttering in front of Poet seemed to make stuttering a good thing for the first time in my life.

The sound of words I had written and that Mr. Spiro and I had just read kept bouncing around the room like a ball on the metal roof of our baseball dugout.

I thought about asking Mr. Spiro if I was supposed to understand everything I had written in the poem. Because I didn't. The words had just picked out where they wanted to go. But I was late on my route and I didn't want to talk anymore because I wanted to hear the words I had just said roll around in my head. I looked for my newspaper bags.

Your cargo is on the porch. And I believe I owe you ninety-five cents and of course your customary tip if you would like to collect now rather than tonight.

I had been so excited about our good conversation that I had almost forgotten about the third piece of the dollar bill.

He handed me the coins from his pocket. From a book on a shelf near the front door he pulled out another piece of the dollar bill. Mr. Spiro's word for the week was *seller*.

As I walked the rest of my route I listened over and over inside my head to the words I had said aloud with Mr. Spiro. I listened to him call me Stuttering Poet.

At Mrs. Worthington's house I put her paper exactly where she liked it.

When I turned the corner at Melrose I saw that neither one of my parents' cars were in the driveway. That was good because it meant Mam was back from wherever she had gone. Back where she belonged.

Chapter Nine

I let out a loud field whoop as I ran through the back door.

Mam was usually cooking in the kitchen or cleaning the bathrooms downstairs at that time in the afternoon but I didn't hear her so I gave her another good whoop. She called down that she was upstairs straightening beds. I could barely hear her. I tore up the stairs thinking that I might recite my poem for her if I could figure out a way to show her how to say it with me but when I saw Mam's face my poem and everything else that had been feeling good left me in a hurry.

Mam's lower lip was busted and fat. Her nose was swollen and whopper-sided. Her right eye was almost closed and her other eye was red where the nice white should have been.

I stood outside my parents' bedroom watching her fluff pillows and pull the sheets tight. I had been talking like it was going out of style all day but the words wouldn't line up inside my head to ask her what had happened. She let me watch her do her chores for a while and then turned to me.

Like I told your Mammy. I just had me an accident. That's all they is to it.

Mam picked up sheets and pillowcases from the floor and hurried to the laundry chute. I followed her still not able to come up with any words to say. Mam always moved at a good speed in her house-work but she was going lickety-split through the upstairs like I had never seen her. She went into my room and started pulling the sheets off both my beds even though I had made mine up that morning. Not like Mam could but even she would have said I had done a tolerable job.

Will you be collectin' tonight?

I nodded even though Mam's back was to me. She spun around and stared me down. I nodded for her again.

I told you all I'm going to. Leave it be.

s-s-s-s-Are you okay?

Looks worse than it hurts. Let me finish up here and then I'll cook us something.

s-s-s-s-Was it Ara T?

Leave it be, Little Man.

When I wanted to I could pester Mam to beat the band but it was clear I wasn't going to get any more talking out of her. When Mam said Leave It Be that was what you did and you'd best not waste any more of her time.

I needed to sort out what might have happened to her so I walked back downstairs to get my glove and an old tennis ball and went out to the back driveway to throw against the garage doors which was always my best spot for hard throwing and thinking. My father had to have the doors painted every other year because of me wearing the paint off them. I picked out a low plank for my target.

Mam may have called what had happened to her busted-up face an Accident but there was more to it. Somebody had hit Mam with their fists. A bunch of times. Hard. Any kid knows you don't get a busted nose and two puffy eyes from falling down.

Mam wasn't one to fall down anyway. When she stayed overnight in my room when my parents were on a trip I would hear her get up and walk around without a light on like she could see in the dark. Mam didn't tell lies but she had her way of keeping a secret. A secret was a secret to Mam. It was locked up tight.

Mam was all the time helping me with everything and I wasn't worth a plug nickel coming up with ideas to help her just like I couldn't figure out what to do for Mrs. Worthington. I was getting tired of my usual way of worrying and needed to come up with a plan to fix things.

The more I thought the harder I threw.

I would be glad to be a grown-up for two reasons. The first reason was that I was hoping to get over my stutter. I knew that some grown-ups stuttered but I also knew that some lucky kids grew out of it. At least that was what the doctor who gave me all my shots kept telling my mother. The second reason was that I would be smarter and could figure out what to do with the feelings down inside me. I wanted to help Mam more than anything and I wanted to help Mrs. Worthington but I didn't have any answers. That was a bad feeling. Almost as bad as stuttering.

A good smell came from the kitchen and my nose and stomach started reminding me how long it had been since I had tasted Mam's cooking.

I had gone upstairs to take a bath without Mam telling me and came back down wearing a clean pair of shorts and nice shirt for collecting. My parents were eating out with friends like they usually did on Friday nights. Mam had a big plate of fried chicken on the table along with black-eyed peas and Smashed Potatoes. They were just regular mashed potatoes but I liked to get that good S in there for starters since it meant about the same thing.

Mam sat down to eat with me. She was mostly just dabbing at her food. It was best for me not to look at her. It hurt to see her banged-up face. All I could think about was taking a nice shiny new baseball that still had all the red and blue writing on it and throwing it as hard as I could right between the eyes of the person who beat up Mam.

I wished that I was going to be throwing papers instead of collecting because I felt like heaving something for sure. I had one more week to go before Rat got home and I was planning on some super-hard newspaper throws.

I asked Mam to let me help her with the dishes but she said to go on and start my collecting so I could get home early. She notched up her voice to make sure I heard her.

You needs to pay this full mind. You be home 'fore dark or you'll have me come looking for you.

I could tell she wasn't fooling.

I went upstairs to get some change from my desk drawer. I looked in my billfold at the three words written on three different corners of a dollar bill.

Student

Servant

Seller

I knew I would get a fourth word next week. I didn't have any clue what word it would be but I had a notion it would start with an S. I wondered if Mr. Spiro knew that S was my favorite sound and letter in all the world. If I had been Napoleon I would have changed that stone with the writing on it so more words would have started with an S. Especially my name.

I must have been thinking hard about Mam's busted-up face because I forgot to be nervous about my collecting when I started out.

When I rang the doorbell at TV Boy's house I found myself having bad thoughts about him. Sitting there in front of his dumb television day after day without any problems. I thought that a dirt clod upside his head or a rock to smash the screen would make him forget about television for a while. I knew it was dumb to have feelings like that and I knew it was because I was so upset about what had happened to Mam. But that was how I felt and I couldn't trick myself out of it.

At one house I said Ninety-Five Cents without stuttering. When I was thinking hard about something else it seemed like I forgot to stutter. But I always remembered it again soon enough.

I walked by Mr. Spiro's house where a few hours earlier I had seen all his books and recited my poem for him.

In my mind it was easy to see him sitting in his big chair reading a book from one of the crates. A book that he had bought in Timbuktu or someplace. He had said the world was in his books and I knew he was right about that for himself but could I find out in books how to help Mam? Or Mrs. Worthington? Could I find out in books about the man who made me with my mother or how to get back my knife from Ara T?

Coming up on Mrs. Worthington's house I was glad to see that the porch light was on and that there wasn't a car in the driveway. The last thing I needed was to be yelled at again by Mr. Worthington or to see Greaser Charles.

I rang the doorbell not expecting anyone to be at home but Mrs. Worthington opened the glass door fast like she had been standing there waiting on me.

She had on her red lipstick. Her hair was up on top of her head in a new way. It looked like she had spent a lot of time putting it in its new place. Her eyelashes curled up again but she had on her usual green housecoat instead of a dress. As soon as she opened the door I could smell she had been drinking her whiskey.

How nice to see my sweetie paperboy.

She seemed to be talking okay. The whiskey hadn't made her start saying her words funny yet.

s-s-s-s-Ninety-five cents for this week. And one s-s-s-s-ninety for two s-s-s-s-more weeks if you want . . .

She pushed open the screen door so fast it almost hit me in the face.

Sure, sweetie. Come in while I get my handbag.

I let the door close without stepping inside.

The whiskey had a sweet smell and so did the perfume that Mrs. Worthington was wearing. The two sweet smells all mixed in together reminded me of parties at my parents' house. If the smell got too sweet and especially if it got mixed in with the mothballs in the attic I would sneak outside and over to Mam's room to get away from it.

Come on in, sweetie. Like I told you.

She held the screen door open for me. I didn't have to think twice about going in to see where Mr. Spiro lived but I wasn't sure if I should go inside Mrs. Worthington's house. I was nervous but I went in anyway.

I expected to see stuff all over the floor and broken furniture and glass but what I could see of the house looked company-coming neat. The front hall was smaller than ours but the woodwork looked just as shiny.

Sit there in the living room, sweetie. I'll be right back with your allowance.

Allowance? Where did she come up with that?

I walked into the living room but as soon as I sat down on the couch the loose change in my pockets started spilling out between the seat cushions. Leaving the coins would make me short on my collections so I pulled up the cushions to start gathering my money. Mrs. Worthington came back in the room with a glass in each hand.

Well look at Mr. Moneybags.

I pulled my hand back like I had been doing something wrong. She put the glasses down on the table.

Anything you find in there is all yours, sweetie.

118

s-s-s-s-Just want what's s-s-s-s-mine.

Don't we all, sweetie. Don't we all. Drink your lemonade now.

Calling me Sweetie once or twice didn't bother me but she was overdoing it by a long shot. I put the cushions back straight and sat down. Mrs. Worthington sat beside me and handed me one of the glasses.

I don't know much about my sweetie except you write the nicest notes and you live in that big house on the corner.

I nodded. I couldn't think of anything else right then that she needed to know.

What grade is my sweetie in?

Then I did something really stupid. About as stupid as anything a kid has ever done. Even though Seventh started with a good S sound I held up seven fingers on two hands. Like a three-year-old would hold up three fingers to show how old he is. I could feel my face turning hot. I was upset for not trying my favorite sound.

Mrs. Worthington pretended to be surprised. She put her hand up to her chest. The hand that didn't have a glass in it.

My. My. You are such a tall boy for the seventh grade.

Half the girls in my class were taller than me because I should have been going into the sixth instead of seventh. And I was stocky but not tall at all. It was plain to me that Mrs. Worthington was acting surprised just for show.

And what does my sweetie like?

119

I was looking straight ahead at the woodwork but I knew that she was looking at me because I could smell the whiskey on her breath.

s-s-s-s-Throwing a s-s-s-s-ball.

OOOOOOH. I bet you can throw it r-e-a-l hard.

She spread out the OOOOOOH like a mouse in a cartoon would. A girl mouse.

Talking about throwing a ball was something I usually liked to do but not today. And Mrs. Worthington was talking slower than when I had first come in.

I watched her gulp down the last big swallow of her whiskey drink but when she went to put the glass back on the table she only got it halfway before it fell to the rug. The glass didn't break like the one on the porch. It just rolled around spilling the nearly melted ice cubes. I thought she would go get something to clean up the mess but she just started talking softly. Almost under her breath.

I don't even know my sweetie's name. Mmmmmm? What's my sweetie's n-a-m-e?

Her voice was a little louder this time. Her sounds were getting drawn out more like mine but the sounds came from the whiskey instead of Gentle Air.

A pencil toss was no good. I was too nervous to find it in my pocket. Gentle Air was a waste of time because I could never make air gentle enough when it came to saying my name. Shouting was no good because I knew I wasn't supposed to shout in a stranger's living room.

A plan for an answer finally came to me. It wasn't the greatest answer in the world but it was the best I could do.

Mam s-s-s-s-calls me s-s-s-s-Little s-s-s-s-Man.

Mrs. Worthington nodded slowly and she was smiling. Her long red hair fell over one of her eyes and she just let it stay there like she was peeping at me.

Mmmmmm. Little Man. I like that.

She sounded for once like she meant what she was saying.

Then she put her head on the back of the couch and fell fast asleep. She was snoring. Not like Mam snored but an uneven quiet snore.

I don't know how long I had been in Mrs. Worthington's house but it was getting dark enough for Mam to start worrying. I sure didn't want her to come looking for me. I got up from the couch.

I looked around to find covers but decided Mrs. Worthington didn't need anything over her in July. I picked up the glass from the floor and put both glasses on a *Saturday Evening Post* on the table. With my hand I wiped off a ring that one of the glasses had made. My mother was always getting on to me about leaving wet rings on tables.

I stood over Mrs. Worthington to look at her like I had done on her front porch.

She was so different now from the first time I had seen her when she thought I had called her the bad word. She had gone to a lot of trouble to put on lipstick and makeup. Some of the makeup from her face had rubbed off. Then I saw that the makeup had been covering up a black-and-blue spot under her right eye. It wasn't swollen as bad as Mam's but Mrs. Worthington had taken a lick on her eye for sure. Maybe Greaser Charles or maybe Mr. Worthington had hit her. If Mr. Worthington could yell at her like he did then he could hit her too.

I said her first name in a whisper.
    Faye.

F was my second best sound behind an *S* because most of the time I could let a little air out under my teeth as I said it.

Mrs. Worthington had pulled her legs up under her like she was trying to fit inside a box. Her head was pushed up against the end of the couch. I wrote Faye on the arm of the couch with my finger. I put the *E* on the end of her name whether it belonged there or not. I wanted her to have all the extra there was.

Her red hair had fallen down over both her eyes. Pretty eyes for sure even though one was black and blue. I watched her breathe in and out some more.

Dark was closing in fast when I stepped out on Mrs. Worthington's porch. Mam would be upset because I was out late. I felt at first like running. Running to Rat's house to turn in my collection money and then running home. I walked instead. It felt like a time to be walking so my feelings would have time to get better situated in my head.

On my way to Rat's house I remembered that Mrs. Worthington had not given me the money for the newspaper. She was the only subscriber on the route who was not paid up.

I stopped under a streetlamp and got out Rat's collection book to put a check by 1396 Harbert. I would go by my house and get the money from my desk drawer to put with the collection money I would hand over to Rat's mother.

That seemed like the least I could do for Mrs. Worthington.

Chapter Ten

On Saturday morning I pitched a good game even though I was a little out of sorts because I had upset Mam the night before by coming in too close to dark.

She had gotten on to me but good and said she had been studying about coming to find me. When I talked back to her by saying I had stayed out after dark plenty of times she said for me to mind what she said because she could feel the Haints nearby.

Mam talked about her Haints when she had a strong feeling that something wasn't right. Mam said Haints were like ghosts. You couldn't see them but you knew they were there just the same.

After the game I threw my route hoping to see Mrs. Worthington sitting on her porch but she didn't show herself. I snugged her newspaper close up to the front door so she wouldn't have to step out in her bare feet.

Turning onto Melrose I saw Ara T pushing his empty cart in the opposite direction from his shed. His cart didn't have much in it and it would take him a while to fill it up. I started wondering if I might have enough guts to check out his secret place to see if I could find my knife. I got a heavy weight inside my stomach when I thought about trying to sneak into Ara T's hideout. It was like the feeling I got in class when I knew my name was going to be called to say something. You know where the weight comes from and what it means but you just get downright tired of it.

I folded my newspaper bags under my arm and ran back up Harbert and then over to Ara T's secret door in the alley fence.

On Saturday there weren't as many cars and buses on the streets and the garbage trucks didn't make their rounds. Ara T's alley was quiet except for the usual dogs yapping and a few gasoline lawn mowers making a racket. I thought I could almost feel Mam's Haints as I eased up to the shed but I kept going.

The secret door to the old shed wouldn't open when I pulled on it. I didn't have a broken-off car antenna like Ara T used but I found a wire coat hanger in a garbage can close by and straightened it out over my knee. The coat hanger was flimsy but I pushed it through the hole in the door and wiggled it around until I heard something fall away inside.

On the top and bottom of the frame I felt for the two long nails that I had seen Ara T pull out. They slipped out without any trouble and the door creaked open on its own. Covering the opening to the shed on the inside was a canvas tarp like the one Ara T kept on his cart. I pulled the heavy canvas back and stepped into the dark.

The place smelled like Ara T. I couldn't see much but the room felt small and tight around me like the cloakroom at school. I hooked the tarp back over the shed door to let in some daylight.

The room was tiny and no mistaking that it was where an honest-to-goodness junkman lived. Against one wall stood old brooms and mops and rakes and axes and shovels that Ara T had probably picked up from all over the neighborhood.

Pieces of bicycles and foot scooters and sidewalk skates were hanging on the walls. Wooden crates on the dirt floor were full of empty whiskey bottles and on a long plank resting on more crates turned up on their ends were three old rusty hot plates wired into an electrical cord that ran along the wall. I followed the cord to a single lightbulb with a small chain hanging down.

The lightbulb was one of those small yellow ones that was supposed to keep bugs away in summer and never did but it chased away the darkness with a dirty light when I pulled the chain.

On a shelf above the hot plates was a bag of red onions and cans of Vienna sausages in different sizes. I had only tasted Vienna sausages once and didn't like them. Mam called them Trash Food. A single bed with the legs sawed off was pushed up sideways against the back wall. Old blankets and coats were piled up at the end of the bed. Memphis got cold enough in the winter but the pile of coats looked like they didn't belong in July. Plus they stunk to high heaven.

Cigar boxes and other cardboard boxes under the bed were filled with bottle openers and broken ice picks. Old light switches. Empty Bugler tobacco cans. Small screwdrivers and pocketknives with broken blades. No yellow-handle knife.

At the other end of Ara T's small bed was a crate with a clean blanket on top that looked like the only new thing in the place. Underneath the blanket I found what must have been Ara T's private treasure. A new-looking camera in a leather case with a burned-out flashbulb still in its shiny holder. Two black handbags that seemed almost brand-spank new. Men's billfolds that were empty except for some school pictures of kids. I recognized some of the kids from my school even though they looked younger in the pictures. A shiny silver cup with fancy letters carved into it. A mirror with a silver handle. Shiny table knives and forks. A ring of skeleton keys. A bunch of shiny Zippos. There was no yellow-handle knife but I recognized the big chrome headlight that had been on my old bicycle. It had to be mine because my old Schwinn was the only kind of bicycle around that had a headlight that big and shiny.

I put the blanket back on the crate. Ara T's room was arranged neat in its own way even though it was filled with all that junk. I decided I could learn something from a junkman about how to keep a room straight.

Neat or not the heat and the stink in the room were starting to make me dizzy and sick to my stomach. I had seen as much of Ara T's place as I wanted to. My mind could see him unloading his cart in the shed and start heating up his cans of Vienna sausage and slicing a red onion with my yellow-handle knife and then lying down on the bed and going through his treasures.

About that time I saw something move under the bed that I first took for a cat but then realized was a big gray rat with a long skinny tail. The rat was dragging one of Ara T's red onions. Big rats were always running around in the alleys behind garbage cans but this rat acted like it belonged in Ara T's secret shed. It wasn't going anywhere.

Time to leave. I turned off the yellow bug light and reached for the tarp to pull it down over the opening when I heard dogs barking and then a cart jangling in the alley. I jumped back into the dark of the shed.

The jangling stopped outside but I didn't move. Then the jangling started up again and I could tell the cart was moving faster toward me.

There was no place to hide in the tiny shed.

I remembered how Ara T had backed his cart into the shed so I eased up just behind the tarp but off to one side. As soon as the tarp moved I would try to slip out the side of the shed door.

I heard the cart outside going back and forth like it might be lining up to come in. Then the cart burst through the tarp and crashed into the back wall. Shovels and mops and hot plates started falling. The person who pushed the cart into the shed was still outside. With the tarp knocked down from the opening I had enough light to see the old doll's head on Ara T's cart.

I knew I was trapped and the longer I stayed in that shed the more trapped I would be. I picked up a short-handled shovel that had been knocked to the ground near me. The end of the shovel was as big as any I had ever seen. Holding it in front of my face I eased up to the door opening. When I heard the first footstep coming toward me I took off out of the shed like my life depended on it.

I hit smelly Ara T somewhere in the chest with the shovel and we both went tumbling. He fell backwards and I went forwards. I somersaulted farther than he did into the alley and that one step was all I needed to get to my feet and take off running like all the Haints in the world were after me.

I didn't stop until I was almost home. I didn't go up my driveway until I had gotten back some of my breath. I saw Mam at the stove in the kitchen so I sneaked in the door that led to the back stairs. I felt so stink dirty that I went straight upstairs to take a bath.

When I came down for supper Mam asked me why I was taking so many baths without being reminded.

s-s-s-s-Just feeling s-s-s-s-dirtier.

You seen Ara T hanging around any?

I shook my head but didn't dare look at Mam because she could see in my eyes when I wasn't telling the truth.

You mind what I said about them Haints being close.

I nodded.

Mam would be coming up to sleep on my other twin bed after she finished in the kitchen. My parents had left early that morning in the plane for one of my father's business meetings in New Orleans and a vacation. They would be gone until the next Saturday.

I tried to make myself think about Mrs. Worthington but Ara T's dark shed and the rat eating a red onion and the cans of Vienna sausages wouldn't leave me be. A kid should be able to choose what he thinks about and to say any word he wants. Neither one worked for me.

During the night I thought I heard Ara T's cart jangling in the alley behind the garage but I couldn't tell if it was him for sure because the attic fan was roaring and pouring in air that smelled of my mother's mothballs.

Chapter Eleven

Mam was asleep in the other twin bed when my eyes opened for good early Sunday morning. I had never woken up before Mam.

The sun was starting to come through the big trees outside and that was good because I still was having a hard time getting Ara T's dark cave out of my mind. I had tried to wash away that dirty feeling in the bathtub the night before but I can scrub something off my skin a lot easier than I can scrub it out of my head.

I came around to the feeling that I didn't care so much about losing my knife because I had plenty of money in my desk drawer to buy a new one. What I hated was that Ara T had tricked me out of the knife and my fifty cents because he probably thought I was just some kind of a dummy who talked funny. The stuttering dummy with the shiny bicycles and a yellow-handle knife.

Mam groaned and turned over in bed. She usually never made much noise but she was still having trouble breathing out of her busted nose. I reached over in my desk drawer and pulled out my billfold that held Mr. Spiro's three pieces of a dollar. Mam moved again.

s-s-s-s-If you're s-s-s-s-awake can we s-s-s-s-talk?

Mornin', Little Man.

The way Mam said Little Man always made me feel good. It was a good way to start the day.

Why s-s-s-s-do you think these three words s-s-s-s-go together? Student. Servant. Seller.

Mam took a while to answer. She always tried to give me her best answer even though I could come up with some strange questions.

I reckon each can be a person.

What s-s-s-s-else?

They all starts with the same sound.

There's s-s-s-s-another word that s-s-s-s-goes with s-s-s-s-them. I'll find it out s-s-s-s-Friday.

Who you finding all this out from?

Mam was already out of bed. She could go from sleeping to wide awake faster than anybody. It wasn't time to tell Mam about Mr. Spiro. I had to sort things out a little more before I shared my new friend with her.

A s-s-s-s-friend . . . in my s-s-s-s-head.

Mam knew that meant that I wasn't ready to talk about it.

When's Mr. Rat comin' home?

s-s-s-s-This Saturday. When I s-s-s-s-collect Friday s-s-s-s-night I'm done.

You worked right hard on Mr. Rat's route. I'm proud of you.

I looked at Mr. Spiro's three special words again.

When I got the fourth word I was going to cellophane-tape all the pieces together and have a full dollar bill. I would always keep it in my billfold and never spend it because I knew the words were somehow more important than money. A plain dollar would buy a malted milk and a Baby Ruth at the drugstore. Mr. Spiro's dollar bill was meant for something more important.

Mam went to my parents' bathroom to put on her Sunday clothes even though she wasn't going to morning church. Mam would never take me to her church on Sunday mornings because she said that was when the preacher talked to the grown-ups. But we would go to the singing part that night. My parents took me to church sometimes but the people never seemed to be having as much fun as they did in Mam's church.

When I came down for breakfast Mam had on her black dress with a white collar under her apron. Her lips and eye were looking better but her puffy nose still made a whistling noise when she breathed.

Make us toast, Little Man, whilst I finish the bacon and eggs.

s-s-s-s-Do you want it s-s-s-s-cut?

You knows we do.

My job was always the toast because I liked to butter it after it came out of the toaster and then cut it on the bias like Mam had taught me. *Bias* was a word I thought a lot about but had never been able to say. Even with a truckload of Gentle Air. *Bias* has only four letters but my dictionary says it has five different meanings. If you get right down to it talking is more complicated than people think. One little word can mean five different things. Once I filled up a whole page of notebook paper by typing BIAS because I liked it so much. When I showed the piece of paper to Rat he said I was losing my marbles.

Mam and I were sopping up the last of our bacon and eggs when she said she hadn't seen my newspaper bags inside the back door where I usually left them.

I got that heavy feeling and bad spaghetti taste in my mouth again. I tried hard not to act out of sorts but Mam knew something wasn't right with me.

I had put down the bags in the alley the day before when I was trying to find something to poke into Ara T's shed door.
s-s-s-s-Left them s-s-s-s-under some hedges . . . s-s-s-s-maybe.

I could tell Mam knew I wasn't telling the whole truth but she let me get away with it.
s-s-s-s-Need to go s-s-s-s-g—retrieve them . . . s-s-s-s-pronto.

I tried to walk out the back door and down the back drive like everything was hunky-dory but when I got to the street I took off running like I was stealing second.

I didn't slow down until the corner of Ara T's alley. My side was hurting and I thought my breakfast might come up. I leaned against a fence to get my breath and to try to calm down. Ara T's shed was about three houses from the corner of the alley. I peeked around a fence to see if the bags were still there on the ground. All the garbage cans in the alley had been moved around since the day before. The bags were gone. I eased forward for a closer look. Nothing.

When I got back home and told Mam that somebody must have taken the bags she asked first thing if I had seen Ara T hanging around where I had left them. I shook my head. Too hard and too quick. Mam gave me that extra long look of hers but I knew better than to open my mouth about anything else.

I would have to ask Rat's mother if I could borrow the extra bags that Rat kept at his house. Losing the bags was not a good way to start my last week on the route.

Knowing that Ara T had something else that belonged to me stuck in my mind and it would be the devil to get it unstuck.

That Sunday afternoon I figured that reading might help me stop thinking about Ara T so I got my Babe Ruth book and went to the back patio. I got more interested in the book after reading that Babe Ruth started out as a pitcher instead of a right fielder.

As I turned a page a granddaddy longlegs spider climbed on the arm of the Wicked Chair and then onto my book. I watched it do its herky-jerky crawl all the way across my open book and then onto the other arm of the chair.

I had gone with Rat to his grandparents' farm last summer where his cousins showed us how to play a game with the granddaddy spiders we always found in the hayloft. The cousins would pick up a spider by one of its legs and ask: Granddaddy Granddaddy which way'd the cows go? If it pointed with one of its legs they would put it down and let it walk away. If it didn't point they would smush it in their hands.

I never played the game with them because I knew I could never say two Granddaddys in a row and at the right time. Rat's cousins thought I was just afraid of spiders.

I picked up the granddaddy longlegs from the arm of the chair and walked over and put it on one of my mother's rosebushes. I liked the funny-looking spiders and was glad I had never smushed one even though it made Rat's cousins think I was a sissy. I made sure I busted Rat's cousins with a dirt clod every chance I got.

When I went back to reading my book a word in the middle of a paragraph almost jumped off the page at me. *Unknown*.

I had seen that word on my birth certificate and wasn't sure what it all meant but I knew I was going to have to change up my way of thinking about the man who I thought was my father.

I ran back over to the rosebush to try to find the spider. I was going to pick it up and whisper as best I could. Granddaddy Granddaddy. Which way'd my father go?

I wouldn't have smushed the spider no matter if it pointed or not. But the spider was long gone.

The only time on Sunday I could get my mind to be still was when Mam and I were at her choir practice that night.

Somebody had hurt Mam and she had been quiet and moving slow all week but she was smiling when she sang with her choir about angels with wings and about going to heaven. Seeing Mam happy always led me into a calmer way of thinking. I sat out on the wooden benches so I could watch Mam. She mostly kept her eyes on the man who was leading the choir but she smiled every time she looked over at me and I gave her back a good smile.

I thought about how Mam never got to go on trips or do anything special because she was always taking care of me and cleaning my parents' house and washing clothes and sewing on buttons. When she did get to leave for a few days she came back with her face all busted up.

On the ride home on the bus I tried to trick Mam into telling me who hit her by asking if it was a sin to get mad at somebody because they had hurt you. All she would allow is how a Vengeful Heart didn't do anybody any good.

Another question I had been wanting to ask Mam came to me. I knew part of the answer but it didn't make any sense.

s-s-s-s-Why do they s-s-s-s-make you ride in the s-s-s-s-back of the s-s-s-s-bus?

We can ride up front if you's wanting to.

I knew that bus drivers would let Mam ride in the front as long as I was with her but that sounded even more stupid.

s-s-s-s-I like to s-s-s-s-ride in s-s-s-s-back but the s-s-s-s-rules don't make sense.

Rules is rules. Don't mean they don't need changing but best to abide by them till they is changed.

I know a kid is supposed to respect grown-ups who make the rules and also respect God who knows how everything is supposed to work but I couldn't get over the feeling that neither one of them was doing a very good job.

Thinking about somebody hurting Mam and then remembering all the stupid rules that Mam had to live by just because of her color made going to sleep a hard job. I guess I had a Vengeful Heart because I could feel it busting like when the stuffing came out of an old baseball.

I put my pillow on top of me to give it a hug but that trick didn't work anymore.

Chapter Twelve

My parents had left extra money for the week so Mam asked me if I wanted to ride the bus to the Overton Park Zoo.

I didn't like going to the zoo as much as I did when Mam first started taking me but I knew she still enjoyed it.

Mam could get into the zoo for free after noon on Wednesdays if she wore her white uniform and went in the gate with me. She couldn't go to the zoo on any day that she wanted to like I could. More silly rules by grown-ups.

We waited on a bench for the No. 5 Crosstown. I didn't beat around the bush.

Why s-s-s-s-can't you s-s-s-s-go to the zoo when you want?

They wants us to be a pair, Little Man. And you know I likes to go with you.

s-s-s-s-Do you s-s-s-s-think it's right?

Not my place to be thinking right or wrong.

s-s-s-s-Don't you get s-s-s-s-mad?

I could tell I had asked Mam a tough question. She was having a time coming up with an answer so I helped her.

I s-s-s-s-get mad when s-s-s-s-kids laugh at me 'cause I s-s-s-s-can't help how I s-s-s-s-talk.

Do it help to get mad?

s-s-s-s-No. s-s-s-s-But I can't help it.

I was going to pester Mam some more with questions but she stood up when she saw the bus coming two blocks away. Mam didn't like to talk about certain things. I guess I didn't either but it was starting to come to me that not talking about something didn't make it go away. The doors to the bus unfolded.

Where you want to sit?

I didn't mind sitting in the back but it seemed to me that it was time for Mam and me to sit up front. I plopped down on the first seat and Mam slid in to the seat beside me. I watched the bus driver to see if he would say anything to us but he kept his eyes straight ahead.

Mam's favorite thing to do at the zoo besides watching the peacocks with the long tails prance around and squawk was to sit on a bench near Monkey Island and watch the monkeys play on trees made out of concrete with fat ropes hanging between them. Somebody who knew what monkeys needed put old rubber tires on the island for them to roll around in.

Mam made up her own names for the monkeys like Mush Melon or Mr. Butterbean so we could talk about what they were doing. When one of the big monkeys chased a little one with a stick to take a piece of watermelon rind away I told Mam that we should name that monkey Ara T. I thought that would make her laugh but she told me not to name monkeys after real people even if it was that no-count Ara T.

Mam knew a lot of the other colored ladies walking around the zoo looking after kids. Most of the ladies wore white uniforms and carried parasols even though they knew it wasn't going to rain. Mam told me how women carried parasols to keep the sun off their heads. The ladies would wave and nod to Mam and call her Miss Avent or Miss Nellie and she would call them Miss Something or Other. Some of the ladies were from Mam's church but they didn't act the same as they acted in church. At choir practice the ladies laughed out loud and joked and cut up but they didn't laugh much when they were in their uniforms at the zoo hanging on to white kids. Mam was the only lady who didn't change. She was Mam all the time no matter who she was with or what she was wearing.

Some of the ladies Mam talked to couldn't have seen her since she got her face busted up and I kept expecting one of them to ask her how it happened or at least how her face felt but not one of them said a word about it. It made me think that they all somehow knew what happened but everybody kept a zipped lip.

We were watching people feed the giraffe when Mam caught an older kid who was by himself trying to feed Mr. Longneck a wadded-up paper cup instead of a handful of giraffe food that you could buy for a nickel at a gumball machine close by. The kid kept waving the cup in front of the giraffe trying to make it stick out its long tongue and take the cup so Mam reached over and jerked the cup out of the kid's hand before he knew what happened.

Mind your own business, old woman.

The kid took a step toward Mam but she put the cup in her handbag and took a step toward him.

You'll not hurt God's animals with me watching. You best be off.

The kid was bigger than Mam. He started not to move but Mam was staring him down and letting him know she wasn't going anywhere.

Then he called Mam a bad word.

He said it under his breath but we both heard it. I don't know if I could ever say the word because it started with a hard N sound. But I know I never would try. Mam gave him a long look. I felt my right hand opening and closing for a baseball to throw. She stared him down until he had moved on a far piece from Mr. Longneck.

s-s-s-s-Sorry he said that.

Names is all it is. Don't mean nothing.

Mam watched the boy until he turned the corner at the zebra pen and then she dropped her head down and snapped her handbag open and shut a few times. She didn't like being called that word.

s-s-s-s-He's a dumb . . .

I couldn't think of how to finish the sentence so I just let it disappear in the air.

Besides the kid calling Mam the bad word he had also called her Old. He would have known better than to call her that if he had seen her last summer when I had gotten stuck in a storm drain near my house.

I had crawled down in the drain to get a ball Rat had thrown over my head. The drain was slimy and I couldn't climb out. The more Rat tried to pull me out the deeper down I slipped. When Rat couldn't budge me he started yelling for neighbors to call for help. Before the fire trucks and police cars could get there Mam had gotten down on her belly and jerked me out of there like I was a puppy dog. The kid trying to hurt Mr. Longneck had been smart to move on.

On the way out of the park I told Mam that we had enough money to get our picture made at the photographer's booth near the ice cream stand. She said for me to go ahead and have mine done if I wanted. When I kept pestering her she told me that the people in charge at the zoo wouldn't allow her to have her picture made with me.

I decided I could stand my ground too. If there was anything good about being a kid who stutters it's that sometimes people felt sorry for me because they thought I had a simple mind and they did things for me they wouldn't do for somebody else.

I went up to the guy that ran the booth and told him that Mam was going to have to go back to her home in California and I needed a picture to remember her by because she had nursed me back to health after me being about to die. I stuttered up a storm when I was telling the tale and didn't even have to make up what kind of sickness I had or why Mam had to come all the way from California. The guy took it hook and line and sinker as Rat liked to say.

I wasn't too proud of using my stutter to trick the guy but it seemed to me every now and then I should be able to get some good out of it.

The man even asked if we wanted to wear some of his costumes he had hanging on the wall so I told Mam to take off her little black hat and I swapped it for a big floppy hat with peacock feathers. I put on a black cowboy hat that came down over my ears. Just like the bad guy in *Shane* wore. The photographer man strapped a double holster on me with fake six-shooters.

Mam looked at us in a mirror.
Ain't we a sight for sore eyes.
s-s-s-s-That's good s-s-s-s-because you still have one.

Mam laughed at my joke and straightened the big hat on my head. Mam hadn't been laughing much since she came back from what she called her Accident. I liked to hear Mam laugh more than anything.

We sat down on an iron bench to have an ice cream cone while we waited on the photograph. When Mam finished her ice cream she pulled out a needle story from her handbag to work on. Mam could sew with a needle and colored thread on cloth like other people drew on paper with a pencil.

The needle story was one she had been working on a long time and the one she always brought to the zoo because it told about Noah and the ark. Even though Mam's animals didn't look exactly like they were supposed to you could tell if they were bears or lions and there was always two of them.

I could see the real lions in their cages from where we were having our ice cream. They paced back and forth behind the bars like they were worried about something or thinking about how to escape.

I had something I wanted to beat around the bush on with Mam.
    s-s-s-s-Are you 'fraid of s-s-s-s-lions?

Mam kept her needle going in and out while she talked.
    We had us panthers at home when I was a young'un. They got a few of our pigs and hens but they never bothered me.
    s-s-s-s-I'm more 'fraid of s-s-s-s-words than lions.

Mam kept going on her needle story but I could tell she was thinking about what she should say to me. She never would let the questions I asked throw her off like it did most people.
    Prophet Daniel went down in the lions' den and his faith kept those lions' mouths shut tight. God will see to it that you find your words.

I had asked for it. And I got it.
    s-s-s-s-But you put s-s-s-s-everything on s-s-s-s-God.

She stuck her needle in the cloth and the cloth went in her handbag and she turned her eyes hard on me like Superman seeing through a brick wall.

I do and will for all my days.

Mam got up from the iron bench and headed for the gate in her fast walk. I ran to the photographer's window to get the picture and then ran after her.

I hadn't meant to upset Mam but I had done a good job of it. I started to tell her I was sorry but figured she knew that without me trying to say it.

On the Crosstown bus headed back home I pulled from my back pocket the picture of the two of us and put it in Mam's hand. I smiled at her. She smiled back and soon enough we were laughing up a storm at the picture. Me with that stupid cowboy hat coming down over my ears and Mam in her hat with the black and green feathers sticking out. I kidded Mam that she looked like a peacock. When Peacock tried to come out of my mouth I forgot to start off with Gentle Air and had to scream the word to get it out. I guess I sounded pretty much like a peacock squawking.

Everybody on the bus turned to look at me but Mam and I were laughing so hard that I didn't take the time to stop and think about getting embarrassed.

When Mam and I got home it was time for me to change into paper-throwing clothes.

I hadn't been paying attention to how hot it was at the zoo. My shirt was soaked through. Mam turned on the attic fan as soon as we got inside the house but the air blowing through my window was like sticking your head out of a slow-moving hot car. I laughed out loud again when I put our good zoo photograph under my billfold and wristwatch in my desk drawer. Mam smiling with her peacock hat on sure enough was a sight for sore eyes.

On my way out the back door Mam was at the kitchen sink washing pots. I tiptoed up behind her and grabbed to untie her apron strings. I yelled as loud as I could so there wouldn't be a chance of any stuttering.

MAM'S A PEACOCK.

Mam whirled around acting like she was surprised when I knew she really wasn't. She flicked her wet hands at me.

I'm gonna whup me a peacock if you don't behave.

Mam was always saying that she was going to whup me but she would have walked barefoot across Egypt before she even thought about spanking me. I liked to hear her say it anyway and I made a promise to myself that I was going to listen in my parents' church and try to understand about how God went about doing things.

When I first learned about praying to God I prayed every night that I would wake up the next morning and be able to talk right. The next day would always come with me stuttering on the first word I tried to say. So I finally gave up on God helping me. I never told Mam I had given up on God helping me because I knew it would upset her.

Chapter Thirteen

Thursday afternoon when I got to the ball field our coach surprised us by calling off practice because he said he had heard the man on the radio say the temperature was going to be over a hundred degrees.

Coach had never called off our practice because of hot weather before. He told us to go home and stay in the shade and drink plenty of water. The afternoon was hot all right but not too hot to throw a tennis ball against the garage and get back to the business of thinking more about Mr. Spiro and Ara T and Mrs. Worthington.

All week my head had been going back to Mr. Spiro's house where the walls were filled with books and then going back to Ara T's shed filled with junk and stolen stuff and all those cans of Vienna sausage and the rat eating a red onion.

Ara T's junk was easy to figure out but Mr. Spiro's books were like a giant jigsaw puzzle when you didn't even know if all the pieces were there. I had remembered how to spell Heidegger but the name was not in the H volume of the encyclopedia at home. Mr. Spiro had said Mr. Heidegger was still alive and I figured you had to be dead to get in the encyclopedia.

Mr. Spiro's house and Ara T's shed were both frightening but in different ways. Ara T's was scary because I knew he had stolen most of what he had from around the neighborhood but at Mr. Spiro's I didn't know if I was smart enough to learn what was in all of the books.

Mrs. Worthington and her red hair. That was the dessert of my thinking.

The tennis ball caught the top edge of the plank running crossways on the garage door and shot up in the air like a pop fly. The ball landed on the flat roof on our house that jutted out from my upstairs bedroom. I hated it when that happened. My choice was either to go up to my room and climb out the window to the roof or get a ladder from the garage to lean against the house. I didn't like to go back inside when I was wet from sweat so I got the long wooden ladder from the garage even though it was hard to carry.

I climbed the ladder to the roof and saw the ball near my window. When I sat down on the windowsill to clean the sticky tar off my shoes the breeze felt good coming into my room. I didn't like to take naps but the heat made it seem like a good idea for a change. I took off my shoes and climbed through the window. I got a towel from the bathroom to put on my bed so I wouldn't get the bedcovers sweaty.

My nap must have come quick because the next thing I knew Mam was telling me to get up because it was time to start on my route.

The deepest shade near the newspaper drop to fold my papers was two houses up into the alley under a tree that grew through a wooden fence. I waited for the truck.

The shade didn't help much on these kinds of Memphis days. The leaves on the big trees just drooped because no air was stirring. Walking in the sticky heat was more like swimming.

I saw Ara T coming up the far end of the alley without his long coat on. I watched him every step.

This was the first time I had ever seen him in just his shirtsleeves. His old coat was piled on top of his junk cart that was filled with a rusted washing machine and something that looked like a chest of drawers without the drawers.

Ara T didn't look the same. He always walked and moved slow like an old man but without his coat you could see the big muscles in his arms. Almost as big as Mr. Spiro's arms. His waist looked small without any kind of a pooch belly that old men usually have. The only reason I had knocked him over so easy when I ran out of his shed must have been because I caught him by surprise.

I asked Mam one time if she knew how old Ara T was and she came back at me with

How old is the Devil?

When Ara T got about halfway up the alley he turned his cart around and started back the same way he came from. That didn't make much sense for a man working in the junk trade. I also saw Big Sack sitting in his truck at the end of the alley and wiping the sweat off his face with a red kerchief. The hot weather was getting to everybody.

The newspaper truck was late arriving at the drop. Some of the carriers had pulled off their shirts trying to keep cool.

When the truck finally came the driver was jabbering to himself as he kicked the bundles out of the back. One of the older paperboys yelled at him.

Stop to get a cold one?

Shut your smart mouth or I'll shut it for you.

The driver wiped the sweat off his arms with a rag from his back pocket. Most of the time the driver would kid with the paperboys but it was too hot for kidding.

The carriers grabbed their bundles and started cutting the straps. I found my three full bundles but my key bundle was missing. I finally found the label stuck in a fence where a carrier named Willie had loaded his newspaper bags on his bike.

Willie was older and bigger than the other paperboys and always wore a black T-shirt and black jeans even on hot days. He had metal taps on the heels of his lace-up shoes. He clicked when he walked.

When he went up to talk to somebody I would see him pull out a comb from his back pocket and start sweeping his long black hair back on the sides. It seemed like he couldn't talk without his comb in his hand.

I left my stack of papers and went over to where Willie was laughing and cutting up with some of the other carriers. They were talking like Daddy-O Dewey did at night on his *Red Hot & Blue* radio show.

You s-s-s-s-got my s-s-s-s-bundle.

All I got was mine.

Saw my s-s-s-s-label where you s-s-s-s-loaded.

Don't be jiving me, man.

You s-s-s-s-got my s-s-s-s-bundle.

I said it a little louder but not so loud as a yell. Willie looked at me and then at the other guys who were heading out on their routes. He started laughing.

You best get your short pants outta here, man, or you gonna be running home to Mommy for sure.

He swung his leg to get on his bike. I grabbed his handlebars with one hand and he twisted them away from me so hard that it slung me to the ground.

I'm telling you, retard. Get lost.

He stood up on his pedals and started out of the alley.

I picked up a good-sized throwing rock on the ground and started after him. I got a feel of the weight of the rock in my hand. I picked out a spot on the back of his head where I could bust him. I cocked my arm and was ready to let it fly. I could see that rock hitting him square in the back of the head even though I still held it in my hand.

Willie looked back at me smiling like a suck-egg dog and when he did his handlebars jerked and his front wheel hit the curb. He went flying onto the concrete sidewalk where he had to catch himself with his hands. He got up quick with his shoe taps clicking on the concrete and jumped back on his bike and started pedaling again while he rubbed his bleeding hands on his jeans.

I dropped the rock. I wondered if Willie had felt what I had seen in my head.

Rat had shown me the telephone number to call if I ever was short on papers but I had left his collection book at home. It didn't matter because there was no way I could explain to the newspaper office over the phone what I needed.

I walked a block up Bellevue to a newspaper rack and stuffed in all the coins I had in my pocket. I didn't have enough money to cover the fifteen newspapers I took out. I looked around to make sure nobody saw me taking out such a big stack.

When I finished throwing my papers I walked home and got more change from my desk drawer. I got on my bike and rode all the way back to the newspaper rack on Bellevue where I crammed in enough coins to make up for the papers I had taken. A lot of extra walking and riding in the heat.

Riding my bike back home I decided I was glad I hadn't thrown the rock at Willie even though he had stolen my newspapers. I think Mam would have been proud of me too. She stood her ground with the boy at the zoo by letting him know to his face that she wasn't afraid of him.

Somehow I was going to let Willie know I wasn't afraid of him either. It didn't take much guts to send a rock through the air to bust somebody in the back of the head. It would take a lot of guts for me to send words in the air to tell Willie what I thought about him.

But I was still glad he crashed his bike.

Chapter Fourteen

On Friday afternoon Mam said she hated to stove up the kitchen with it being so hot but that she had in mind to bake a deep-dish pie for my parents who were coming home Saturday.

I was on my last day of the route and then Rat would be back to take it over.

Mam told me she was going to the grocery store later on and might still be out when I got home from throwing papers. Mam usually had the groceries delivered when my parents were away but when she called the store to place her order the grocery man told her the delivery boy had taken off because the heat had made him so light in the head that he couldn't ride his bicycle.

We'll eat us a late supper after your collectin'. Too hot for a body to eat at five o'clock anyhow.

We s-s-s-s-can s-s-s-s-celebrate.

That's right, Little Man. You had you a fine July throwing all those newspapers. I know Mr. Rat will be glad to see you.

Rat would let me go with him and throw the paper route any time I wanted but I was going to miss doing the route on my own even if it was a hundred degrees and some of the other paperboys didn't play by the rules.

❖

At the newspaper drop the driver called out my bundle number.
　　Rat's s-s-s-s-back tomorrow.

The driver looked at me and nodded. It wasn't often I gave out information without being asked.

I went over to slick-haired Willie who was folding his papers and stuck my bundle label in his face.
　　That's mine.

I said it in a loud voice to cut down on my chances of stuttering. I spread my feet a little and was ready to take whatever he had to offer. Willie surprised me. He looked at me and gave me a half of a smile.
　　Take it easy, man. Everything's copacetic.

I liked the way he said *copacetic*. Rat had heard the word on the playground and thought it was something dirty but I told him it just meant that everything was okay.

A month before I wouldn't have said anything to Willie. I would have just kept my mouth shut and stewed about him taking my bundle. The route was changing me.

I didn't know if I was going to tell Rat about standing up to Willie or about all my good conversations with Mr. Spiro. I knew I couldn't tell him about Mrs. Worthington. At least for a while. Rat wouldn't tell anybody else if I made him swear on the Bible not to but I wanted to keep what happened for my own until I understood it better.

I had looked for Mrs. Worthington every day but she was staying inside with the door closed even in all the heat.

I was full of good throws on my last day of the route. End over end. Side arms. High shots. Low shots. Curves around posts. I even threw one through a porch railing. The folded newspaper split the small opening slick as a whistle and came to rest against the house. I didn't miss one porch.

I was counting on my last night of collecting being just as good as my last day of throwing.

❖❖❖

In my room I picked out my best shorts and a clean shirt in case I might get to see Mrs. Worthington.

I knew Mam had gone to the grocery store because her little black hat and parasol were gone from the hall tree at the foot of the back stairs. It felt strange to leave the house without Mam there but strange feelings had been coming in bunches the whole month of July.

The first surprise of the night was seeing TV Boy out on the porch swing when I skipped up the concrete steps to his house. I figured it must be too hot for even him to be inside with his nose stuck to the screen.

When I rang the doorbell his mother told me to wait on the porch while she got some change. TV Boy was swinging and looking straight ahead into space.

s-s-s-s-Nothing on s-s-s-s-television?

He acted like he didn't hear me.

What s-s-s-s-do you watch all the s-s-s-s-time?

Not one word from TV Boy.

His mother came out of the door about that time and handed me the correct change. Then she did something that knocked me off my rocker. She turned to TV Boy and started moving her hands fast like she was a third base coach giving him signals.

She was talking to him with her hands.

TV Boy said something back to his mother by moving his hands and then got out of the swing to go inside. When he stepped through the door he turned around and smiled at me. I smiled back. Two kids don't have to say words because they can say all they need to sometimes with their smiles.

I remembered going with my father to his office and riding up on the elevator to his floor. The elevator man looked at my father when we got on and then my father pointed at me and back to him-self without saying anything and the elevator man smiled at me. When we got to his office my father said the man was a Deaf Mute meaning that he couldn't hear or talk. My father told me that he was a nice guy and if I ever met anyone like him I should never call them Deaf and Dumb. He said this guy was just as smart as everyone else except that he was born not being able to hear or talk.

I thought about TV Boy as I walked from house to house and felt bad about getting mad at him the week before. Just like I couldn't help it that I stuttered it wasn't his fault that he couldn't hear or talk. Being able to hear is nice but I wanted to tell him that he wasn't missing anything by not being able to talk.

I decided TV Boy would make a good friend. He wouldn't have to hear my bad talking and he could teach me how to say things with my hands instead of my mouth. I was pretty sure I would be good at that kind of talking because my baseball coach always said I had good hands.

The street names in blue tile on every corner left me with a lonely feeling as I walked my route for the last time. It was like saying goodbye to friends.

I thought about how Mr. Spiro's route had taken him to countries all over the world but these few Memphis streets had been my whole world up until now.

I was an eleven-year-old kid standing on a street corner in Memphis in short pants. I felt like I was so small that I would be blown away if the slightest puff of wind came up.

But you didn't have to worry about any kind of a breeze showing up on a late July afternoon in Memphis.

Chapter Fifteen

When I had delivered Mr. Spiro's paper earlier in the day the front door had been closed as usual but at collection time it was propped open with a crate of books.

Mr. Spiro's old bicycle with the rusted handlebars was on the porch leaning up against the house. The basket on the front of the bicycle held something that looked like a canvas sack with straps on it. I stuck my head in the door and called out for him instead of ringing the doorbell.

Mr. Spiro answered from the back of the house.
Be there in a moment, Messenger. Do come in.

I listened in my head again to the way he put the Do before the Come In. He could add one little word to a sentence and that word would make all the words more important.

Inside the house some of the crates of books had been moved around with more crates sitting in the middle of the floor.

But the room didn't feel right to me.

A white duffel bag like the one our team carried bats in was on the floor with clothes and books beside it. CONSTANTINE SPIRO was printed on the white bag in faded black square letters. Beneath the name was SS *Patrick Henry*.

I didn't like what I saw. My father's packed bags on the bed always made me feel bad and Mr. Spiro's duffel bag was giving me a double whammy to the stomach.

Mr. Spiro came into the room with a small green bottle in his hand. He poured a little of what was in the bottle in his other hand and began patting his face and neck. He was in khaki pants and a T-shirt so white and clean that it looked like Mam had just washed and ironed it.

Lilac de France. The best antidote in the world for close quarters belowdecks.

Mr. Spiro was smiling and his voice had an excited sound.

You're going away?

The words spilled out of my mouth before I could think about stuttering. Even the G sound that usually stopped me dead in my tracks.

An investigative reporter you are. Yes. I'm going on a short excursion but I'll be back in the fall.

Where?

Early tomorrow I'm catching a tow headed up the Mississippi and then I'll take my bicycle and jump ship somewhere in the Badger State. Wisconsin.

I felt like being a smart mouth and telling Mr. Spiro that I had learned all the way back in the fourth grade that Wisconsin was the Badger State but I could feel myself getting upset and everything clogging up inside of me. When I didn't say anything Mr. Spiro kept on talking.

The Seven Seas and the Seven Continents have long been my ports of call and now I want to explore the Seven States of the Great Lakes.

I didn't like the way Mr. Spiro kept saying Seven. Seven was my favorite number and a number I could say most of the time. Mickey Mantle wore No. 7. I saw a green scoreboard with a seven beside Mr. Spiro's name and a big fat zero beside my name. I tried to keep myself from looking too down in the dumps because it was plain to see that Mr. Spiro was excited about his trip and all his sevens. But covering up my feelings when something got sprung on me was another thing I wasn't very good at. He stood in the middle of the room studying me and patting his face with a white towel he had pulled out of his bag.

I had considered leaving earlier in the week on another tow up the Mississippi but I wanted to make sure we had a good conversation before I left. And . . . we have some unfinished business.

My stutter always got worse when someone threw me a curve like Mr. Spiro had just done with his packed bags. Sure I wanted to know about the fourth word but I wanted to calm down inside and wait until I could talk better.

s-s-s-s-Could I s-s-s-s-do the rest of my s-s-s-s-collecting and then s-s-s-s-come s-s-s-s-back?

Certainly, Messenger. That'll give me a chance to get shipshape here. I'll be expecting you forthwith.

I gave him the best smile I could come up with and backed out the door.

I had come around to thinking that Mr. Spiro was the only person I could talk to about my father not being the man who made me with my mother. I had planned on asking him if I could still visit him each week even after I was done filling in on the route. And now Mr. Spiro was packing a bag on me.

I put down check marks in the collection book at each house but my marks weren't as neat as they had been at the start of July. If Rat didn't care about throwing papers the right way or keeping his route book neat then I didn't care either. I had thought that my last Friday night would be my best night but it wasn't working out that way.

At Mrs. Worthington's house the driveway was empty but the porch light was on which made me think she might be waiting for me. I wanted to talk to her one last time or maybe not talk so much as look at her again up close.

As I reached the top step I saw a white envelope clothespinned to the screen door. Written on the outside of the envelope in a nice hand was the word *Paperboy*. My hands were shaky like just before throwing the first pitch of a game because I had the feeling that whatever was in the envelope would either be All-The-Way Good or All-The-Way Bad.

I didn't have my knife to slit the envelope so I sat down on the porch swing and opened it as neat as I could with my fingers.

A five-dollar bill was folded around a note written in a woman's curvy hand with big loops on the capital letters.

> *Please cancel our newspaper. This should cover what we owe.*
> *Thank you for your excellent service.*
> > *1396 Harbert*

I put the note in the collection book and the five-dollar bill in my back pocket.

All the grown-ups around me were making things hard for me all at once like they had gotten together and planned it.

Before I could think what I was doing my finger pushed Mrs. Worthington's doorbell. The chimes gave me a start when I heard them and I jerked my hand away. My feet wanted to run but I needed to see Mrs. Worthington. I rang the doorbell again. No lights came on inside. The house was dark and quiet.

I sat down on the porch swing and looked at Mrs. Worthington's note again. Her handwriting was nice with even spacing between the words and the sentences didn't go uphill or downhill even though there weren't any lines on the paper. I had the feeling that she had taken a lot of time writing the note but I knew it wasn't really what she wanted to say to me. I think she was apologizing for inviting me into her house. She was disguising what she wanted to say just like Mr. Voltaire said.

I got up from the swing and started home.

Halfway home I picked up a good throwing rock. There were plenty of glass streetlamps shining at me. The fat lights made good targets and I could feel my arm getting ready to haul off and bust one and make the glass come down like rain but there was also the Man in the Moon peeking out through the clouds and the heat. The Man in the Moon was giving me a suck-egg smile.

I threw the rock at the moon. As hard as I could throw. I found another rock. And another one. I threw so many rocks that I was out of breath and my arm was hurting.

The Man in the Moon was still smiling and laughing at the boy way down below who thought he could hit the moon with a rock.

Chapter Sixteen

When I started up the driveway to my house my head finally got back to the business of the paper route.

Rat's mother was expecting me to come by with the collections so Rat could pay his monthly newspaper bill when he returned the next day. I hadn't collected Mr. Spiro's money yet so I needed change to make up the difference. I also needed some money to pay for the bags Ara T had stolen. I could have used Mrs. Worthington's five-dollar bill but I wanted to keep it in my pocket a little longer.

Mam was stirring a pot on the stove. The kitchen was sticky hot even at seven o'clock at night.

s-s-s-s-Need to get some s-s-s-s-change. s-s-s-s-Going to Rat's and s-s-s-s-then I'll s-s-s-s-be back to eat.

I was using Gentle Air to beat the band. It was the only way I could get my words out with my head dancing around so much. Mam looked at me.

Everything okay, Little Man?

s-s-s-s-Just tired of the s-s-s-s-p . . . s-s-s-s-Tired of the route.

You hurry and gets your change and then get on back from Mr. Rat's 'fore dark.

I was so out of sorts I didn't even look to see what Mam was cooking.

The best breeze in the house late in the day was on the back stairs when the attic fan sucked the air up the dark stairway.

I sat down on the landing and switched my thinking to Mr. Spiro. His packed duffel bag was stuck in my head. I still couldn't believe he was leaving on his trip. I wanted to ask him questions about my Unknown father and hear him talk about his books and things he had seen while he was traveling around the seven continents. Everything he talked about was new and soap-clean. And he was going away on a towboat for more adventures and I was stuck in this hot stove of a city with only Rat who would tell about what a great time he had on the farm and how many dirt-clod fights he had with his cousins and how he wished I had been there to help him.

I was glad for Rat but all the work I had done on the paper route for the month had left me with nothing but three words on a cut-up dollar bill. I did want to know what the fourth word was so I hurried on up the stairs. I knew Mam was still worrying about her Haints and she wouldn't let me leave the house after dark.

The curtains in my room blew toward me as I walked down the hall but even with the fresh air coming in the room I could tell that the smell wasn't right.

My room was all out of whack. The drawers under both of my twin beds were pulled out. That didn't make any sense because the only stuff in them was blankets and sheets and winter clothes. The next thing I saw was the chair pulled away from my desk and all the drawers hanging open. Mam had taught me never to leave drawers open. Especially the middle drawer with all of my money in it. It was pulled out so far that it was tipping down in front.

A bad feeling came over me like it did at school when the books under my desk were not in the same order I had left them.

The money was gone from the drawer. All of it. My billfold and my wristwatch too. The air from the attic fan coming through the window was hot but I let it blow over me until I could get what had happened in my room straightened out in my head.

When I went to the top of the stairs and yelled for Mam she heard something in my voice more than just my words because she came up the stairs two at a time. We ran down the hall together.
    s-s-s-s-Gone. s-s-s-s-Money's gone.

Mam stopped in the middle of the room and breathed heavy.

Even though her nose was busted. Even though my mother's moth-balls from the attic smelled. Even though the air coming through the window was new and hot. Mam smelled the same rotten smell I did. Ara T.

Mam went to the desk and jerked it away from the window like it was made out of model-airplane wood. She leaned out the window and looked at the flat roof.

Did you leave that ladder up?

I nodded.

When I s-s-s-s-got my s-s-s-s-ball yesterday.

Mam pulled her head in and jerked the window down so hard that the weights on the ropes banged inside the wall.

Mam untied her apron while she walked down the hall. She may have been walking but I had to run to catch up with her. She draped the apron on the post at the bottom of the stairs which was the first time I had ever seen it not hanging in its place on the back of the pantry door.

I can't leave you here, Little Man. You get right on up to Mr. Rat's house and wait for me there.

She looked at me for a nod.

Mam turned off the stove eyes and grabbed her black pocketbook from the pantry. I followed her out the door and down the back steps. Even as fast as I could move it was hard to keep up with Mam.

Even more strange than where she put her apron was seeing her leave the house in her white uniform without her little round black hat.

Mam stopped at the end of the driveway.

You get on up to Mr. Rat's now.

I didn't move or say anything.

Listen to me strict now. I've got some business that's mine alone. You mind me now and get on up to Mr. Rat's house.

I turned away from Mam and started walking up Melrose. Slow as I could walk. She went the other way in her fast walk. I knew she would make a line straight for Ara T's shed.

When I came to the corner to turn onto Rat's street I looked back and saw Mam was almost to Ara T's alley. A new plan came to me. I watched Mam head into the alley and then I took off running back down Melrose.

I ran so fast I couldn't hear my tennis shoes hitting the sidewalk. I turned up Harbert just before I got to Ara T's alley and kept running up the street past Mrs. Worthington's house. Three houses from the end of the street I cut into the driveway and ran beside a wooden fence that came out near Ara T's shed.

Before I reached the alley I heard Mam yelling for Ara T. A few more steps and I was in the alley. Mam was pounding on Ara T's secret shed door. Some of the door's chipping gray paint floated to the ground like snowflakes. Snowflakes in Memphis in July.

Mam pulled at the shed door but it was locked tight. I started wondering if I should tell her how I had seen Ara T open it by pulling out the two nails on the side and sticking something through the small hole. Right then Mam reached up and grabbed the top of the shed door with her hands. She gave the door a yank with all her might. The door came loose from its hinges and crashed to the ground with splinters and gray snowflakes going everywhere.

Mam stepped into the doorway and threw back the tarp covering the inside of the shed. The yellow lightbulb came on and I heard shovels and rakes falling and crates being emptied. Then a few seconds of quiet. Mam came back out the door of the shed and stood in her white uniform with her hands on her hips. She looked straight at me like she knew I had been there all the time.

You disobeyed me.

I was ready for whatever Mam had for me because I was going to tell her that I wasn't leaving her. I was going wherever she was going next and there wasn't anything she could do about it.

She seemed to know what the inside of my head was saying.

You have carfare money?

I patted my front pockets and felt the coins and wadded-up bills from the night of collecting. I couldn't spend any of that but then I remembered Mrs. Worthington's five-dollar bill in my back pocket. I pulled it out and handed it to Mam. She took off down the alley with the door to Ara T's shed lying flat on the ground and the yellow light still shining. My mother always liked to say that Mam would walk barefoot across burning coals to turn off a light.

We turned on Bellevue and walked the one block to Peabody and past the paper drop where I had folded newspapers all month. I thought about how all the paperboys would be at the drop the next afternoon handling their papers and cutting up with Rat and asking him about his month at the farm. The paper drop was empty. If I had been by myself just seeing that spot would have given me the lonelies but Mam and I were headed for some business with Ara T. Walking faster and faster.

We crossed Peabody to a bus stop where Mam usually would hum a church song while we waited. She stepped back and forth on the curb trying to spot a bus.

Where we s-s-s-s-going?

I knew most of the answer but it seemed like I needed to ask the question anyway.

You know Ara took your money and your things and I'm going to get 'em back. Right quick like.

I had never heard her call Ara T just by his first name.

My first thinking was to say not to worry about the money and that my father would just fill the desk drawer again with change from his pocket but thinking about Ara T with my Ryne Duren card and the photograph of me and Mam at the zoo and especially Mr. Spiro's words written on the three pieces of a dollar bill stirred me up on the inside.

The bus was empty when we stepped on. Mam handed the driver the five-dollar bill and then she gave me the change to put in my pocket and sat us down on the first seat on the side opposite the driver. He gave her a look but Mam spoke before he could say anything.

Do this car cross Lauderdale?

The bus driver said it did.

Mam stared straight out the front window of the bus with her two hands holding the top of her black handbag like somebody might try to yank it away. Mam had been in her white uniform all day. Had cooked breakfast and lunch in it and walked to the store and back with groceries on this hundred-degree day and her uniform was still white and morning fresh.

The one thing Mam did on the bus that surprised me was to open her handbag and take a pinch from a bottle of Garrett's with her thumb and finger and put it in her lower lip.

Mam had never taken a dip of snuff in front of me.

Where did your yellow-handle knife come from?

s-s-s-s-Don't know. s-s-s-s-Just always had it.

You'll have it again, Little Man, and all your other stuff. Don't you be worrying.

Chapter Seventeen

Mam stood up a full block before we got to Lauderdale and pressed
against the front doors of the bus instead of pulling the overhead
cord and going out the back like we usually did.

She held my hand waiting for the bus door to hiss and fold open.
Mam had not done that in a long time.

We walked down streets that were new to me. I read the signs.
Lauderdale. Beale. Linden. Pontotoc. Vance.

I didn't know Vance came downtown so far. The two-story houses
on this part of Vance looked like they had been nice houses a long
time ago but most of them had old cars parked in the dirt yards and
sofas and chairs with the stuffing coming out lined up on the front
porches. Men were sitting on red Coca-Cola cases turned on their
ends and women were fanning themselves with pieces of cardboard.
Everybody was laughing and talking loud and looking like they

were having a good time. The people in my neighborhood would all have been in their houses at that time of night with the attic fans blowing but everybody in this part of Memphis was outside and stirring.

We came to a store with a glass front that was bright on the inside and full of whiskey bottles. The rows of bottles looked like books lined up on library shelves.

We kept walking down Vance with Mam stopping to pop her head in the small stores and places with music playing.

More Juke Joints 'round here than the law should allow.

What's a s-s-s-s-Juke . . . s-s-s-s-Joint?

Where the choirs of the devil sing.

Some of the signs on the stores were lettered in a bad hand with the words misspelled. When we got to the corner of Vance and Orleans Mam made sure I knew her rules in this part of town.

No matter what, Little Man, you stay close. If I tell you something, there won't be any disobeying. You hear me?

I nodded. Double.

Mam turned the corner at Orleans and started walking back toward Union Avenue. She stopped dead still at the first alley we came to. In the back of a small red building were a bunch of junkmen's push-carts with their handles sticking out. Mam tightened down on my hand as we walked down the alley toward the red building.

A bare lightbulb over the top of the back door of the building lit up the jumble of old carts full of the usual junkman's junk. Mam shoved one cart out of the way to get a better look at one in the middle. No mistaking. It was Ara T's cart with its tarp and plastic doll head and all the shiny foolishness tacked on it.

Mam stood straight with her hands on her hips looking at the other carts and sizing up the red building. I could tell that she was making a plan. Before Mam did anything big at home like taking the rugs out to beat them or waxing the wood floors she would always stand with her hands on her hips to come up with how she wanted to go about things. When she was finished making her plan she would start in on her work and never miss a beat until the work was finished.

Mam squeezed my hand tighter when she moved closer to the back door of the building. She cupped her left hand to her ear and leaned against the door. The alley was quiet so it was easy to hear the music inside the house. It sounded like a woman singing but then the song ended and another one started up and I could tell then it was just a record playing. People were talking and laughing inside and bottles and glasses were clinking together.

Mam moved back closer to Ara T's cart and pulled up the old tarp.

Listen to me strict now. Take my pocketbook and crawl up under here. Don't you peep out for nothin' or nobody.

Climbing up in Ara T's smelly old cart was not something I wanted to do but I knew I didn't have a choice if Mam had her plan worked out. I stepped up on the handle and then slipped under the tarp. Mam covered me.

Be back directly, Little Man.

She patted my head like she always patted my foot when she left my room at night.

I couldn't tell if Mam had been gone for five seconds or five minutes. I hadn't moved a muscle under the tarp because I was listening hard and could hear only car horns honking and a few sirens every now and then.

The heavy canvas and the cart smelled as bad as Ara T did and without getting any of the little breeze from the alley it was getting harder to take a full breath. I counted to ten in my head saying Mississippi after each number.

1ne Mississippi

2wo Mississippi

3hree Mississippi

4our Mississippi

5ive Mississippi

6ix Mississippi

7even Mississippi

8ight Mississippi

9ine Mississippi

10en Mississippi

I know that's not how you type numbers but that's how I see them in my head because I can't separate the numbers and the words. I counted to ten again. And again.

I was sweating and having trouble getting my breath. I couldn't stay under the tarp any longer. It was time to get out and go see about Mam. She would just have to be upset with me because staying in that cart was making me sick to my stomach. I needed air even if it was the sticky summer Memphis kind.

I saw by the light of the single bulb on the building that I had been lying on Rat's two canvas newspaper bags I had left in the alley near Ara T's shed. I thought about Rat who would be coming home the next day and then I thought about Mr. Spiro and his merchant marines and how much I would like to have both Rat and Mr. Spiro and all his marines with me now. But they felt a gazillion miles away.

I eased up to the door of the red building and cupped my hand to my ear like Mam had done. A record was playing like before but there was not as much talking or clinking glasses. I looked for a doorbell but then decided that it wasn't the kind of place to have one on the back door. Or the front door. Holding Mam's black handbag as tight as I could I opened the door and stepped inside.

The place was darker than the alley and the thick smoke from cigarettes made it even harder to see. The smell was not as bad as inside Ara T's cart but close. I walked on my toes with my hand against the wall through a narrow hall that led to the front of the building where the music was coming from. The song on the record confused me at first because I thought it was a song that I remembered Mam and her choir singing about Letting Your Light Shine. It didn't seem right that they should be playing a church song in a Juke Joint but when I listened closer I figured out that the song was talking about letting your Love Light Shine and that was a different kind of light and probably a different kind of love from the kind Mam sang about in church.

Just then a man in a shiny blue shirt came running lickety-split down the hall toward me. I plastered myself against the wall and he zoomed past me and out the back door. If he saw me he didn't let on.

The narrow hall was dark but the room that opened up in front of me had colored lights around the walls like you see at Christmastime on front porches. As I walked through the door everyone inside the room was standing at their tables staring at something on the far wall. The record about the Love Light was still playing but everything else was quiet.

My eyes started getting use to the dim light. At an empty table near the middle of the room I saw my brown leather billfold. Scattered around it was a pile of paper money and coins. I went a little closer and saw Mr. Spiro's three pieces of a dollar and my Ryne Duren card and the picture of me and Mam at the zoo. The rest of the table was covered with glasses and brown bottles and sliced up red onions and opened cans of Vienna sausage. Ara T's stinky coat was hanging on the back of a wooden folding chair.

The thing that everybody in the room was staring at was Ara T in a torn shirt and his old hat holding Mam up against the wall with both of his big hands around her throat. Mam's white shoes were dangling with her toes pointing down trying to touch the floor. When she tried to hit Ara T in the face with one of her fists he spread his elbows like a chicken wing to block her arms. Even as strong as Mam was and as good as she was with both of her hands she couldn't get in a solid lick.

A man in a fancy red hat standing at one of the tables picked up a wooden chair with both hands and eased up to Ara T's back. He lifted the chair to his side to swing it but Ara T saw him and grabbed the chair with one hand and smashed the chair on the man's head. Pieces of the chair went everywhere and the man backed away. Ara T still had Mam pinned against the wall with one hand. He held a piece of the chair in his other hand.

Mam's white uniform was whiter than white in the dark room. Her arms were spread out and flapping. She looked like one of the angels on the front of the songbooks at her church getting ready to fly to heaven.

With his chewed-up cigarette in his mouth Ara T was cussing loud at Mam and then laughing and then letting out a cry that sounded more like an animal at the zoo than a human. Ara T never had a loud voice when he talked to me in the alley but it sounded like he was talking into a loudspeaker for everyone in the red building.

I'm killin' this bitch this time.

Ara T then screamed into Mam's face.

Just likes I killed your skinny-ass brother.

Mam was still swinging at him with her arms but I could tell her strength was leaving. Something was oozing out over her lower lip that I first thought was blood but then saw was her Garrett's. She didn't see me because she was looking straight into Ara T's eyes. Not like she was afraid of him but like she was trying to come up with a plan even though time was running out.

That was when my plan came to me.

I put Mam's handbag on the floor at my feet and reached with my right hand for a brown bottle with a long neck on the table next to me. The people at the table didn't see me because they were standing and watching Ara T choke the life out of Mam with one hand and swinging the piece of the broken chair with the other.

The bottle was empty and the neck was wet and slippery. I wiped it off with my hand and then I wiped my hand on my shorts until my right palm was good and dry. I felt the weight of the bottle. I opened and closed my fingers around the neck until the bottle was balanced just where it needed to be. The neck of the bottle fit my hand like it was made for it. Better than even a baseball or a newspaper.

Ara T's dirty hat against Mam's white uniform made a perfect target. I held the bottle above my right ear and spread my legs for balance putting my left foot out ahead just a little. Just like my newspaper throws.

I cocked my arm. In my mind I could already see the brown bottle flying toward Ara T's head.

I yelled as loud as I could. So loud Mr. Spiro could have heard it in Timbuktu. Vowel sounds aren't my best but this one came blasting out of my mouth and no stutter in the world could have stopped it.

ARA T.

At the same time I said his name I let fly with the bottle. As hard as I could throw. Even harder than throwing rocks at the moon.

The bottle came out of my hand in a perfect end over end.

I should have thought about the way Ara T's floppy hat sat high on the top of his head. If I had taken dead aim at his ear the bottle would have caught him between the eyes and dropped him right there on the spot but it hit him on the top of his head when he turned toward me. The bottle knocked his hat flying and then hit the ceiling where it crashed with a loud pop. Brown glass sprinkled down on Ara T and Mam.

Ara T dropped his hand from around Mam's neck and the piece of chair in the other hand fell to the floor. He had opened his mouth when the bottle hit him and his crooked cigarette had fallen out.

Mam slid down the wall with her hands clawing at her throat and gulping for breath. Ara T rubbed his forehead where the bottle had smacked him. He staggered a little but got his balance quicker than you would have thought after taking a bottle to the head.

He grinned and started toward me and I saw his gold tooth shining like the headlight on my Schwinn.

I probably could have made it out the back door of the building without Ara T laying a hand on me but I couldn't take my eyes off Mam leaning against the wall pulling at her throat.

Ara T reached out for me with his big sweaty arms. Still grinning his crazy grin.

Looks like I'm gonna breaks me a white boy's neck now.

Ara T's voice was booming and his gold tooth shining. I saw for the first time that the reason the tooth was so bright was because there weren't any other teeth around it.

If you were just walking into the room and saw only his face you would have thought Ara T was smiling and kidding around but if you were up close looking into his wild eyes you would have known he was serious.

Ara T's extra-strong junkman's hands closed around my neck. The next thing I saw was my watch around Ara T's wrist but he had it on upside down. That bothered me and then I decided I had more to worry about than how he was wearing my watch.

I managed one good kick at his knees because I knew he would block my arms but he pinned my legs against a table with his body. His red eyes were wide open like some monster in a comic book. His gold tooth was shining in the dark of his mouth and his breath smelled like it was on fire. Vienna sausages. Red onions. Cigarettes. Whiskey. All that was missing from my list of worst smells in the world was my mother's mothballs.

My eyes wanted to close but over Ara T's shoulder I saw Mam get to her feet and wobble toward Ara T's old coat hanging on the back of the chair. I worried that Mam was thinking about just throwing the coat over Ara T's head and that probably wouldn't do us much good because Ara T was getting a grip on my neck like you grip down on a baseball bat at home plate. I thought I knew what being strangled felt like because I choked on my words all the time but this kind of choking made me want to close my eyes and just go to sleep. I could barely see Mam but could tell that she had started moving faster.

In my mind I was trying to tell Mam that she needed more than Ara T's coat and then I saw her jerk something out of one of the pockets. I didn't see her open it because she did it in such a quick move but then I saw the shiny blade of my yellow-handle knife slash across Ara T's arm that was closest to her. On the bias. Ara T let out a quick yelp and grabbed his sliced arm with his good one.

Mam backed up a half step to get a better balance. Then she yelled.
    PHILISTINE.

The word came out different than a field whoop but just as loud. Whatever the word was she meant it.

At the same time she switched the knife to her other hand in one quick move for a better angle and plunged the blade into Ara T's other arm. All the way in. Up to the yellow handle.

The knife went in as easy as when Mam opened a ripe watermelon on the kitchen table. Ara T could whet a knife better than anybody.

Mam motioned for me to get behind her as she backed away from Ara T. The blood had begun to ooze from around the yellow handle. Ara T let out another animal sound and started toward us and that was when I heard a commotion from behind and something lifted Mam and me to the side in one motion like we were checkers on a checkerboard.

Big Sack.
   It's done, Ara.

Ara T looked up at Big Sack and then reached down for a piece of the chair that had fallen to the floor. With the arm that didn't have a knife sticking in it he raised the stick of wood over his head and swung it.

Big Sack caught Ara T's arm at the wrist. He gave a twist and the piece of wood fell to the floor. Big Sack gave another twist to the arm and I heard it pop like when I threw a hard one into Rat's catcher's mitt.

Ara T's eyelids closed and then he dropped to the floor. Not like how cowboys fall down in movies but like when a coat falls off a hanger and crumples.

❖❖❖

The phonograph record had finished playing but it was still going around with the needle making a scratching sound.

Big Sack started telling people what to do but he wasn't talking fast like he was nervous.

Get me that gin bottle, Silk.

A guy in a blue shirt grabbed a half-full bottle and handed it to Big Sack who emptied the bottle on Ara T's bleeding arm. It came to me straight then that Silk was the one who had run by me earlier to get Big Sack.

Hold him, Silk.

Big Sack wrapped a white handkerchief around Ara T's arm where the knife had gone in and grabbed the yellow handle with the other hand. He yanked.

Ara T's eyes opened and he rose up to let out a yell that had no match anywhere in the zoo then slumped back down on the floor. Blood gushed until Big Sack put down the knife and tied the bloody handkerchief tight around Ara T's upper arm. Big Sack grabbed Ara T's old coat and wrapped it around the bloody arm too. He turned to Silk.

Pull Ara's wagon to the door and bring his cloth.

Where we takin' him, Big Sack?

They'll be shootin' dice in back of Hatty's. We'll roll him there and get him stitched.

Mam left my side and walked around Ara T's head. She picked up the knife from the floor and wiped the blood from the blade on a sleeve of Ara T's coat and slid my watch off of his wrist. She stood to face Big Sack.

You knows I had a right.

None said you didn't, Miss Nellie. It's done. You best clear out with the boy.

Mam folded the blade in and put the knife in the pocket of her uniform with my watch.

Big Sack knelt down and gave more orders.

Get a mop and rags from back. And some motor oil and sawdust. Fix a record on that player. Show here's over.

Everyone watched Mam as she reached down to pick up her black handbag I had brought in.

She took the yellow-handle knife and my wristwatch from her uniform pocket and put them in the handbag and then walked to the table in the middle of the room. She moved the glasses and bottles to one side as easy as if she was clearing the dishes in our dining room after supper. She pushed my coins into a pile like she did with peas after she had finished shelling them and raked all the coins into her handbag. She carefully picked up the three pieces of Mr. Spiro's dollar bill and our photograph and my Ryne Duren baseball card. She put everything in my billfold and put the billfold in her handbag. Mam snapped it shut like she wanted everybody to know that everything was over and done with like Big Sack had said.

Mam put her arm around my shoulder and we started for the back door as calm as if we were leaving choir practice on a Sunday night. We walked past Big Sack who was sliding Ara T onto the canvas tarp that Silk had brought in. Even down on his knees Big Sack was looking me straight in the eye.

Ara T won't bother you again, Little Brother.

I nodded because I took Mr. Big Sack to be the kind of man who meant what he said.

As we walked outside past Ara T's cart I reached in and got Rat's newspaper bags.

I wanted to look back through the open door of the red building but I wasn't going to if Mam didn't. Mam had done a needle story about a woman in the Bible leaving some bad city and when she looked back God turned her into a block of salt. I don't know if the story was real but I wasn't taking any chances.

Mam didn't say the first word until we were on the Union Avenue bus by ourselves.

We'll talk in the morning whilst the house is empty. You lay back and rest easy now.

I nodded but wasn't sure I could do much resting. Mam held her hand-bag in her lap with both hands on top. She looked straight ahead.

As we got closer to our stop I remembered I had missed out on Mr. Spiro's fourth word. That word was important to me. Whatever it was. And once I missed out on something like that I knew I hardly ever got a second chance.

Chapter Eighteen

I wasn't surprised the back doorbell buzzed so early the next morning. I looked at my wristwatch that Mam had put on my desk. It was six o'clock. But it seemed to me that the Memphis police should have come to the front door.

The only people that buzzed at the back door were the grocery boy or sometimes Rat if he couldn't see Mam in the kitchen. But six o'clock in the morning was too early for Rat to be back from his grandparents'.

I decided I would just stay in bed until the policemen came up to my room to handcuff me and take me and Mam to jail. I wondered if they would be in blue uniforms or if they would wear coats and ties like the two *Dragnet* guys on TV who always talked like they were reading out of a book.

The police would ask me questions and I would start stuttering up a storm and telling them I didn't remember anything because I was so scared and maybe they would feel sorry for me and Mam and let us out of jail after a few days. Fact was I could remember everything about the stabbing like it was a movie that kept running over and over in my head.

I must have turned the movie into dreams because when Mam called up to my room it was after eight o'clock.

You gonna sleep to noon up there?

I smelled sausage frying so I put on clean shorts and a shirt and went downstairs.

Who was at the s-s-s-s-back door?

Nice man on a cycle.

Mam always pronounced it Sickle like in Popsicle.

He said he owed for the paper. Said he wanted to pay 'fore he left town.

Mam handed me the envelope from her apron pocket. I could tell it had more than coins in it. I folded it in half and stuck it in my back pocket instead of running upstairs to my room to open it. Mam always said I liked things to simmer a bit.

Mam poured a tall glass of cold milk to go with my sausage and eggs and biscuits. Mam usually didn't make biscuits on Saturday morning but there was a plate heaping high on the table next to a bowl of sausage gravy. I hadn't eaten anything since lunch the day before and Mam knew that her biscuits and sausage gravy would fill me up if anything would. She poured herself a cup of coffee and sat down at the breakfast table in the chair across from me. She hooked her thumb around the spoon that always stayed in her coffee cup.

You eat and let me talks a spell.

I could tell that Mam had been thinking a good while about what she needed to talk to me about.

What happened last night shouldn't have, Little Man. We're going to talk about it this one time and then never again for all our born days.

She looked at me for a nod. I gave her one. And then I promised again with my eyes.

She went back to the beginning and told how she had known Ara T when she was growing up in Mississippi. He lived with a family who worked on the farm next to the one Mam's family worked on. She figured Ara T was about five years older than she was and told how he was all the time getting into trouble by taking stuff that didn't belong to him and picking on kids smaller than he was. Especially her brother. The two had gotten into fights and her brother always watched Ara T plenty close when he came around. She said most everyone was afraid of Ara T because he would fall into the fits without any warning. The only one who wasn't afraid of him was Big Sack who lived on another farm near Coldwater.

On the night her brother died Mam heard a scream on Coldwater Creek that ran between her house and Ara T's. Her brother had been to town to sell eggs so he could buy flour and sugar for her family. When they found him in the creek the sack of flour was scattered up and down the banks but the bag of sugar was gone and Mam's brother was dead.

Mam's father always suspected that Ara T had killed his son for the bag of sugar but never could prove it. Later on Ara T left Mississippi to come to the city. Mam had been in Memphis almost a year before Ara T started coming around our neighborhood. She told him to keep away from our house but he said the alleys were his and he could go where he pleased because Memphis was a Free State. Mam said she had asked Big Sack to keep his eye on Ara T. Big Sack told her the day he came to our door that he had seen me hanging around Ara T.

Mam got up to get me some more sausage gravy from the stove.

Will the s-s-s-s-police come?

The Memphis law don't pay much mind when harm comes to somebody like Ara T.

Why did s-s-s-s-Big Sack say that Ara T would never s-s-s-s-bother us again?

Big Sack is a man who makes things right. He'll see that Ara T moves on. Ara T knows not to buck Big Sack.

Will s-s-s-s-people in the red s-s-s-s-building who saw what s-s-s-s-happened tell?

Some will talk in the devil's places. But nothing will come of it. People know Ara T got what was due him.

s-s-s-s-Will you tell the s-s-s-s-police what Ara T did to your brother?

Mam explained how her people cleaned up their own messes and didn't depend on white people and their police. She said her people had always done it that way in Mississippi and then in Memphis and it always worked out best like that.

Mam told me to ask all my questions because when we got up from the table Ara T would never be talked about again.

s-s-s-s-Was Ara T the one who s-s-s-s-busted your face?

She nodded.

I caught him comin' out of his alley shed and told him to keep away from you . . . and I told him I knows what he did to my brother.

s-s-s-s-When did he s-s-s-s-bust you?

I told him I's going into his shed to find your knife and he spun me around and hit me. I gots in a couple of good licks but he bested me . . . that time.

I asked her if she thought she was going to die when Ara T had her slammed up against the wall with his hands around her neck.

I fear no man the likes of Ara T. No matter who has hold of me I know the Lord will protect my soul.

I had asked my mother one time after church to explain what a Soul is and she said we would talk about it when I got older.

s-s-s-s-What's your soul?

Your soul is the part of yourself that nobody can see. But it's the best part of a body's life because God has control of it.

I had more questions about the Soul but I knew it had to do with the Bible and I was going to have to think on that more before I could ask the right questions.

I asked her how she knew my yellow-handle knife was in Ara T's coat pocket. She said she had felt the Lord himself move her to the knife with a sure hand and she knew what had to be done.

Where's the s-s-s-s-knife now?

Buried so deep the Hounds of Hell can't dig it up.

I sat at the table while Mam sipped her coffee. My mind went back to the night before. I could see Ara T's hands around Mam's neck and then feel them squeezing my throat. I could see the yellow-handle knife slash and then go deep into his arm. I could see the blood ooze and then begin to spurt.

The tears started from deep behind my eyes without me knowing they were coming and then came gushing out like water out of a busted pipe. I never cried much but I couldn't turn these tears off and stopped trying after a while.

Mam sat at the table with me until I emptied my eyes. She smiled when I wiped the last tears away.

You threw that bottle with a mighty heave, Little Man. Just like David.

I remembered Mam's needle story about the boy who busted a giant with a rock from a slingshot.

I was glad I had a bottle to throw. I'm not as good with a slingshot.

Chapter Nineteen

Summer heat waves in Memphis usually end with thunder and lightning and rain that floods up over the curbs but the hot spell on the first Saturday in August broke a little after noon with a puny drizzle.

The breeze coming in my window was just how I liked it. I sat at my desk with the envelope Mr. Spiro had given Mam. I opened it to find three quarters and two dimes for the week's *Press-Scimitar*. And the last piece of Mr. Spiro's special dollar.

I opened my desk drawer where the night before Mam had put my billfold and all the coins and paper money she had brought back in her handbag. I took the three pieces of the dollar and put them together in the desk drawer so the breeze from the attic fan wouldn't blow them away.

Student

Servant

Seller

I took the fourth piece from the envelope.

Seeker

Mr. Spiro's dollar was complete. I was glad the word started with an S like I knew it would.

I found my cellophane tape in another drawer and taped the dollar bill to make it whole. The four pieces of the dollar bill fit together perfectly. I put it in under a flap in my billfold that was supposed to be a secret compartment. Most billfolds had them so it wasn't much of a secret anymore.

The last thing in the envelope was the piece of paper I had typed my poem on. Mr. Spiro had written something on the other side.

Dear Brave Traveler,

I am disappointed we missed our business transaction last night. When I return after the autumnal equinox, we will explore more in depth what I have found in my studies. Until then, Messenger, continue to raise your unique voice and write your poetry as you seek to understand the quartering of the soul.

Constantine Spiro

P.S. Please have Arthur hold my newspaper until my return.

I read the letter three times. I knew Mr. Spiro was trying to give me a clue to the four words on the dollar bill. Mr. Spiro's leaving felt better because he had left me something to work on and because he told me when he would be coming back. I also liked that he talked about the Soul because I was going to spend a lot of time thinking about that.

◆◇◆

The back door buzzer sounded and soon Rat came clomping up the back stairs.

He was tan without any sun lines on his neck or arms. Going without a shirt was another treat on the farm except at hay baling time and then you better have your shirt on or you would have to take a dip in the pond with the cows to stop the itching.

Rat told me about the dirt-clod fights with his cousins and trying to catch baby rabbits while his grandfather cut hay with the tractor. I listened and tried to think about what he was saying even though I was having a hard time keeping my mind on his stories.

How'd the route go?

Good-good.

Why don't you throw the route with me today? We can each take a bag and I'll walk instead of ride.

I didn't want to disappoint Rat on his first day back home. Rat would be telling stories about the farm and I would try to be excited with him even though I had an idea that stories about dirt-clod fights and catching rabbits wouldn't be that interesting anymore.

When we reached the paper drop the bundles were already on the ground and carriers were loading their bags. Rat pulled out his double-bladed Barlow to cut a bundle cord.

Where's your knife?

s-s-s-s-Lost it . . . somewhere.

Maybe you'll get another for your birthday.

He tried to wink like he wanted me to know that he might be planning on giving me a new knife from his father's hardware store. But he wasn't very good at winking with one eye.

We each put a newspaper bag across a shoulder. I gave Rat the route money for the last week and we went over his collection book as we walked. I wanted to make sure he knew where everybody stood on their newspaper bill. When we got to Mr. Spiro's house I told Rat that he was paid up and that Mr. Spiro didn't want a newspaper delivered again until the autumnal equinox.

When the hell is that?

Rat always cussed a lot when he got back from being with his farm cousins but he would stop right quick the first time his father heard him.

September twenty-second.

He scrunched his nose at me.

s-s-s-s-Looked it up.

When we reached Mrs. Worthington's house I told Rat that the address was paid up but that she wanted the paper stopped.

Why?

s-s-s-s-Don't s-s-s-s-know s-s-s-s-but I got a tip.

Good. I never got anything from those cheapos.

s-s-s-s-Lucky me.

I looked back at 1396 Harbert with the overgrown privet around the porch and wondered if I would ever be able to tell Rat about Mrs. Worthington. I don't know what I would tell him. I didn't understand it myself except I thought Mrs. Worthington was the prettiest woman I had ever seen. And the saddest.

When we finished the route Rat asked if I wanted to throw ball but I told him that my mother always expected me to take a bath before they got home from a trip.

I wanted to tell Rat all that had happened to me and how his paper route had changed me but the parts of the story I could tell didn't make sense without the parts I couldn't tell.

When my parents came home later that afternoon I was on my bed reading the *Press-Scimitar* about the Yankees beating the White Sox 3 to 1 with Ryne Duren getting the save. A picture in the paper showed my favorite pitcher lighting a cigar for Casey Stengel the manager who was having a party on his sixty-ninth birthday. Ryne Duren was having a good summer on the mound.

My mother came upstairs first. She handed me a small box with see-through plastic on top.

I brought you your favorite. Pralines with pecans.

She always made a big deal about buying me pralines even though I didn't like them. I guess she thought if she liked them then I must like them too.

She asked how my last week on the route had gone and I told her the heat had been pretty bad. She said the heat in New Orleans had been Unrepenting. I guessed she meant Unrelenting.

She went on about how their hotel in New Orleans was air-conditioned and said that she and my father had been talking about having someone build us a new house way out in East Memphis with air-conditioning. She said it would be near a private school that I would like and that the house might have a swimming pool.

I told her the attic fan suited me just fine so she said we'd talk about it later. That was the code for We Won't Talk About It Later.

I had made up my mind to crumble up the pralines and throw them on the roof for the pigeons to eat but when she was about to leave I handed her the box.

s-s-s-s-Thanks . . . but . . . don't like s-s-s-s-pralines.

But I always thought . . .

s-s-s-s-Never have liked s-s-s-s-pralines.

She gave me a strange look. I was expecting her to say Everybody
Likes Pralines and I was going to say I'm Not Everybody. But she
took the box and left the room.

My father came up the stairs carrying his heavy suitcases with Mam
behind him carrying my mother's. My father never let Mam tote his
suitcases even though she probably could have lifted more than he
could. My mother told Mam to come in the bathroom and help her
sort dirty clothes. Mam would be washing and ironing for the next
two days. I walked down the hall a ways.

What's gotten into that boy of mine, Nellie?

What you mean?

He seemed upset that I brought him pralines. I thought he liked
them.

He just be growing up, Mrs. V. Don't worry 'bout him. He's
gonna be fine.

My father came into my room after he had finished unpacking. His
right hand dug into the front pocket of his suit pants.

Is the bank open on Saturdays?

I opened my desk drawer and watched him dump in a week's worth
of loose change.

How did your week go, son?

s-s-s-s-Hot. s-s-s-s-But okay.

How about the collecting?

He didn't ask the question just to be talking. I could hear the real question in his voice.

s-s-s-s-Everything worked out okay.

Hard work deserves a bonus . . . and I believe you have a birthday soon.

He pulled some folded paper money out of his front pocket and took a twenty-dollar bill from the top. He stuffed the bill into my billfold. He didn't see Mr. Spiro's taped-together dollar in the secret compartment.

Wow. s-s-s-s-Thanks.

I started thinking Ara T had missed a pretty good payday by just a day. Twenty bucks would probably have kept Ara T in whiskey and Vienna sausages and red onions for a good long time. Then I remembered I wasn't supposed to be thinking about Ara T.

My father picked up my ball glove from my bed.

Rain's about stopped. How about some pitch and catch before dark?

I knew the last thing my father wanted to do after flying his plane all day was pitch and catch with me. I wasn't much interested in throwing ball either. I still felt empty with all my tears gone. But I pretended that pitching ball was just what I wanted. So both of us ended up doing something we didn't really want to so we could make the other feel good.

We put on our ball gloves and started throwing in the back driveway trying to keep off the wet grass.

I had been coming around to a new way of thinking about the man playing pitch with me.

If he had been the man that made me with my mother then he would have had to be a father to me no matter what. Even if I stuttered or looked like the Lizard Boy on the midway at the Mid-South Fair. But since my father wasn't the one who made me with my mother he could have said I wasn't of his doing and he wouldn't have had to raise me or make time for me. It seemed I owed him a lot more than I owed somebody who I didn't even know. I wasn't sure I even wanted to learn anything about the other man because he didn't want to know anything about me as far as I could tell. I figured there was a good chance that he didn't even know he had a part in making me.

My father on the birth certificate might have been Unknown but the tall man throwing ball with me in his white shirt with his necktie stuffed between the buttons was my father as far as I was concerned. He got his shiny dress shoes muddy when he stepped in the flower beds to get a ball. He always tried to do about everything in the world for me and he didn't even have to if you wanted to be official about it.

The speech teacher my parents hired had told me that stuttering was what happened when a person tried extra hard not to stutter. I wondered if that was why I stuttered around my father more than anybody. I could tell he worried about me and I wished I could get over my stutter for him as much as for me.

I picked through a couple of words that started with an easy H so I wouldn't have to hiss out a bunch of Gentle Air.

Handle some hard ones?

You bet, son. Let me have 'em.

Then I did something strange. Even for me. I threw my father four good pitches without him even having to move his glove so much as an inch. With each throw I called out one of Mr. Spiro's four words.

Student.

Servant.

Seller.

Seeker.

My father put his hand to his ear after I made the last throw.

What's that?

s-s-s-s-Just some s-s-s-s-good words.

Looking back I guess I was trying to tell my father about the four special words in the best way I could think of. If Mr. Spiro's words were going to help me to figure out things that I needed to do then maybe the words would help me pay back my father for being so good to me. I had it in my mind that if I put each word on a ball and sent it flying straight to him that my father would have them forever the same way I would have them in my billfold.

I know it sounds stupid but I'm glad I did it.

Chapter Twenty

The best thing about junior high school is that I get to change class-rooms for every subject.

My math teacher told us on the first day that we'd be working with Unknowns. It doesn't seem fair to pile more Unknowns on top of all the Unknowns I already have. But that's the seventh grade for you.

On the second day of school Rat was in the cafeteria line with me when I saw the meat was Vienna sausages wrapped in bread. The menu on the blackboard called them Pigs in a Blanket. I told Rat I wasn't about to eat one.

Why?

Just s-s-s-s-can't eat s-s-s-s-those things.

Why not?

s-s-s-s-They look like s-s-s-s-dog turds in a s-s-s-s-blanket.

Rat told another guy at our table what I said and the guy sneaked up to the blackboard and erased Pigs and wrote in Dog Turds. Soon every guy in the lunchroom was laughing and woofing like a dog. Not me. I didn't want to think about Vienna sausages anymore.

I've only walked down the alley behind Harbert one time since school started. The door to the secret shed was leaning up against the fence and everything was cleaned out down to the smallest piece of junk. I wondered if the rats ate the red onions.

I didn't go to the Mid-South Fair even though Rat and Freda wanted me to win a big stuffed animal for them on the midway by knocking over milk bottles with my throws. Rat has started dating Freda except he calls it Going With Her. I think that's funny because Rat's father has to take them everywhere they go.

Rat thinks Freda is some kind of a hot tamale even though she's lived three doors up from him all his life and he never paid much attention to her before. Rat said Freda wanted me to start calling him Art and she wants him to get rid of his crew cut and start growing his hair long like Elvis did before he left Memphis last year and went into the Army. Rat said I should grow my hair long too and I told him I would keep my crew cut because I had plenty of things to think about instead of combing my hair all day.

I've started spending time with TV Boy in the afternoons when he gets home from his special school. His mother taught me how to say a few words with my hands but TV Boy and I don't really need to talk when we're around each other. We like to look at baseball cards and play Pick-Up Sticks since we're both pretty good with our hands.

I found out the reason that TV Boy watches so much television is because he's learning how to read lips. He even tries to read my lips which is probably extra-hard practice for him.

TV Boy's real name is Paul. *P* is easy to make with your hands because all you do is point with your index finger and touch your middle finger with your thumb. No Gentle Air needed.

I've only seen Mrs. Worthington once since school started.

Walking home from Paul's house late one afternoon I turned the corner and there were Mr. and Mrs. Worthington walking ahead of me on Melrose. They were holding hands and swinging them like girls on a playground. They were acting happy but whether they really were or not I couldn't say. I kept watching as they walked away from me. Mrs. Worthington had cut her hair. I could still see her in my mind on the couch peeking at me with one eye from behind that pretty red hair. But it was gone now.

Mam and I have been talking more now about things ahead of us instead of things behind us.

She saw me reading the sports pages in the *Press-Scimitar* last week and asked me what I was going to do to earn a living when I got older. When I was a kid I thought I would grow up to be a pitcher for the Yankees but something tells me I'm not going to end up in the big leagues. I've decided that throwing a baseball is what I like to do only because it's important for me to be good at something.

Mam asked me who wrote all those words in the newspaper and I told her it was the people who had their names at the beginning of the stories. She told me I should work at a newspaper because I can write well. I think she was talking about my handwriting and how much I liked to type and not about how the words are put together but I think working at a newspaper is something I might like to do. Since I can't get words out of my mouth the right way maybe the thing for me to do is to learn how to put them down on paper. The only bad thing is that I would have to start using commas.

Most nights before I go to bed I pull out my billfold with Mam's goofy-hat picture in it and Mr. Spiro's special dollar bill. I've started carrying my billfold in my back pocket along with some paper money but I make sure Mr. Spiro's taped-together dollar stays hidden. I won't ever spend it or give up trying to understand what the four words mean just like I won't give up on trying to get rid of my stutter.

My parents talk a lot more about the new house in East Memphis that they're going to have somebody start building for them. They show me wide pieces of rolled-up paper and explain how the garage will be Attached and how Convenient the new washing machine and clothes dryer will be. My mother goes on about how she wants one of those new central vacuum systems that's built into the walls of the house. When I asked my mother where Mam was going to live she said that We Would Talk About It Later.

Rat's mother came by yesterday afternoon. It was the first time she had ever been in our house so I knew I needed to listen in from the landing on the stairs even though I had promised Mam I would stop eavesdropping so much.

Rat's mother had a copy of the *Press-Scimitar* which had a story on the first page about how more schools in Arkansas were going to start making all kids go to class together no matter what color they were and even though it caused such a big problem two years ago that the Army had to be called in. My mother said it wouldn't be too long before all the schools in Memphis were Segregated. Rat's mother allowed as how she meant Integrated and my mother told her it was all the same thing. I felt sorry for my mother. I don't know if it's worse not being able to say words at all or being able to say them and not know what they mean.

When they were walking to the door Rat's mother said she and Rat's father had started thinking about moving out to the country so Rat could go to a school that they knew would be full of only white kids.

I still don't see why it's such a big deal to have everybody going to the same school. You can't tell what a kid is like just by how he looks. Or how he talks.

I'm almost finished but I have one last thing to type.

This morning my homeroom teacher said that since there were so many new kids in class she wanted each of us to stand up row by row and say our name and tell something interesting about ourselves.

We sat in alphabetical order so that meant I was one of the last kids to stand. I was expecting to start getting nervous about saying my name and then commence with all the twitching and sweating and maybe running out of the room pretending I was sick or shaking my head and refusing to say anything. But all on its own my brain took off and started doing something new.

My mind floated up out of my head and I could see myself down below standing in front of the class like I was the teacher. Sitting in the desks were the people from my summer.

Mam. Mr. Spiro. My father. My mother. Rat. Willie. TV Boy. Big Sack. Mrs. Worthington. All of them listened to me while I talked.

I told Rat I was going to start calling him Art like Freda wanted.

Mr. Spiro was sitting at the front with his eyeglasses down on his nose and I was saying a poem for him. He was directing me with his hand like I was in Mam's choir. But Mr. Spiro wasn't saying the words with me.

I told my father and mother that I was glad I belonged to them no matter how I got there. I told my father I wanted us to try to work on what Mr. Spiro's four words meant. Just the two of us. We could do that instead of playing pitch and catch so much. I told my mother that I wouldn't get mad at her anymore and I would help her find the right words to say if she wanted me to.

Willie was combing his hair and I told him that we were Copacetic. He laughed and then pointed down to what he was wearing. Short pants and tennis shoes.

I told TV Boy that he was my best friend behind Art. Paul understood every word I said.

Big Sack was standing beside his school desk because he was way too big to sit in it. I told him I trusted him to take care of me as much as I trusted my father and Mr. Spiro. He called me Little Brother again in his quiet voice.

Mrs. Worthington was putting her hair up on top of her head in swirls. It was longer and brighter red than ever. I told her I knew that the only reason she talked to me so much was because she had been lonesome and needed somebody to talk to. I told her I knew exactly what that felt like and that she was still the prettiest lady I had ever seen and I wanted her to be happy even if I couldn't be her paperboy anymore.

Mam was on the back row in her starched white uniform and wearing her round black hat but when I looked at her she got her pocketbook and came to stand with me at the front. I told her how glad I was that she had come to live with us and I thanked her for saving my life.

Just before it was my turn to introduce myself to the class my mind dropped back down into my head.

When I got up from my desk seat, all my classmates turned to look at me.

My name is Victor Vollmer the Third. I stutter when I talk but I like words anyway. I also like to play baseball.

I stuttered about the same as always with all the gigantic pauses and funny sounds coming out around the words but I didn't pay any attention to how my classmates looked at me and didn't try to figure out what they were thinking. And I said exactly what I wanted to.

I sat down. Art was looking back at me and smiling from his desk in the front of the room. The real live Art. He gave me his funny wink with two eyes.

Mam had a plate of peach fried pies waiting for me when I got home from school. I put my books on the back stairs and went to the ice-box and got a bottle of milk. Mam had my glass on the table and I poured it full.

How's school today?

s-s-s-s-Good. Want to s-s-s-s-know what I learned?

Sure do.

s-s-s-s-It's more important what I say than how s-s-s-s-I say it.

You right about that, Little Man.

s-s-s-s-And my soul doesn't s-s-s-s-stutter.

Mam smiled and went back to her cooking. Humming a choir song. She didn't say anything but I knew she understood.

I'm done typing now.

I'm going to tie up these pages tight with newspaper cord and go out back and bury them under the loose bricks in the patio under the Wicked Furniture.

I know I'll have to dig a deep hole to keep the Hounds of Hell from getting to them. Words in the air blow away as soon as you say them but words on paper last forever.

Author's Note

"One of the hardest things in life is having words in your heart that you can't utter."

James Earl Jones, noted actor and the resonating voice of Darth Vader, spoke those words because he knew the pain of a stutter as a young person. Through hard work and perseverance, he was able to gain control of his speech, turning his voice into a magnificent tool.

The names of famous people with speech problems are legion, but for every well-known actor or world leader who has battled a stutter, there are millions of us who live the drama on our own small stages. The Stuttering Foundation of America estimates that more than 3 million Americans and 68 million people worldwide deal with speech impediments. Stuttering affects three to four times more males than females.

Stuttering manifests itself most cruelly during childhood, creating a lonely and baffling existence just at a time the world is beginning to open and expand.

My first recollection of my stutter is just before I was five. I have been stuttering—sometimes fiercely, sometimes gently—for more than sixty years now. Despite my impediment, I had a rewarding career in newspapers, and to my continued amazement, I enjoy telling my story to audiences, especially young people.

Have I been cured of my stutter? No. Have I overcome it? Yes.

Paperboy takes place in 1959, when modern speech therapy techniques were in their infancy. Great strides have been made in this field over the last fifty years, but there is much more work to be done; there are many more questions to be answered and a wealth of confounding riddles to be solved. Through the wonders of DNA exploration, scientific evidence is mounting that stuttering is hereditary.

For those who want to learn more about this disability, I offer three excellent resources:

- The Stuttering Foundation of America (stutteringhelp.org)
- The National Stuttering Association (nsastutter.org)
- The Stuttering Home Page (mnsu.edu/comdis/kuster/)

I also invite you to read my *Notes from a Stuttering Expert*. This paper, written for the Fourteenth International Stuttering Awareness Day Online Conference, speaks to those who stutter, as well as to their parents, friends, and family and to speech clinicians and pathologists (mnsu.edu/comdis/isad15/papers/vawter15.html).

Paperboy is my story, then, certainly more memoir than fiction. While the novel's protagonist deals with an all-consuming speech difficulty, he also learns that life is about much more than stuttering.

Questions and comments are welcome at vincevawter.com.

Vilas Vincent Vawter III, age eight